SOUL
FLAME

Cover Art: Chris Law
Cover Design: Adam DeDobbelaere
Author Photo: TJ Devadatta Best
Editors: Marcy Llamas Senese and Patricia Harriman

www.theholistichousehold.com

Library of Congress Control Number: 2017913250
Heart Check Publishing, Del Mar, CA

ISBN 978-0692938676

I'm about to let go of everything. Everything I've ever known. Everything I've ever wanted. My Jeep climbs higher and higher up the hill to our neighborhood that overlooks the city. What is happening to me? Am I actually going to do this? Something stirs deep inside of me. Then I feel a laugh begin. It erupts from my throat, loud and untamed. Pure elation. I bang on the steering wheel, the freedom releasing in my laughter, the tears flowing from my eyes. I catch my reflection in the rearview mirror.

I already know the answer.

CHAPTER 1
THE SEARCH

We are driving through the suburbs, in his 4-wheel-drive truck, searching for a home. There's a country song booming through the speakers and his strong hand is gripping mine. I have layers of clothes on and a heated coat because this winter is supposed to be one of the coldest in Western Pennsylvania history. It is certainly the coldest winter I have ever experienced in 28 years. The snow falls as we pull into the driveway of a dark-colored house with a suburban feel and a tiny bit more seclusion than most of the homes in this area.

Having grown up in the city, he is the one looking for seclusion. I had land to run on for miles and miles so the city is still an okay choice for me. But I'm compromising because, well, why not? I've finally found a man I'm compatible with who's ready to settle down, start a family, make a life. And he wants to do that with me.

"This could be the one," he tells me. We peek into the windows of a house that looked a little better on the computer screen. I walk around to the sloped backyard with a small patch of trees. Could this be where we live? Where we start a family?

"What do you think, Morgan?"

Any doubts I have about the house become eclipsed by what I feel about Nick.

I've searched a long time for Nick. I may not have realized what I had the first time we dated because it took me three years to find my way back to him. He's handsome, funny, generous, healthy and we have similar interests and career paths. Striking blue eyes, dark hair, a huge smile and a solid, muscular body—Nick stands out in any crowd. Plus, there's a toughness to him that I like that could only have come from learning how to survive from an early age on the streets of Pittsburgh where kids stole his bicycle and he had to fight to get it back. Where his father taught him how to hold his own. To a wounded puppy like myself, a man who offered this type of security felt really, really good. He was loud, he was opinionated and he knew what he wanted. He was a kind person but he was not to be crossed. He gripped my hand as we walked across the street. He watched for me as I got any further than arm's length. And he paid for our comfortable lifestyle. He was a man's man with a doctor's credentials and a sensitive side. He was exactly what I had been looking for.

Even though my dad had doubts about us getting back together, he actually liked him. My mom liked him too because her daughter was now safe, sound and taken care of. The consensus of those closest to me was that of relief. We weren't really sure if I was capable of settling down and maintaining stability, but now, somehow, it looks as if I'm pulling it off. I'm even surprising myself with the vigor with which I can wash someone else's clothes, do someone else's grocery shopping, and essentially be a "good girlfriend." I am even helping him open up his new office where I will soon be employed. It seems as if all the pieces are falling into place. House hunting is part of the perfect picture.

"Look honey, only one mile from the office." I point to a cookie-cutter house on the screen with the same granite, stainless steel look equated with success. I try to focus on the granite instead of the fact that the house is lodged right up next to Route 79.

The real estate in Barraine sells quickly even though it is situated right in the middle of nothing, landlocked with no body of water anywhere in sight. It is home to every strip mall, chain restaurant and otherwise cliché housing development man has to offer. Classic suburbia with below freezing winters and more days of grey clouds and rain than imaginable.

So I have one major request when it comes to our new home: a garage. Six month winters + a skinny little girl who sometimes cries scraping ice off her car in the morning = garage. Also several vacations in the winter. If I can't vacation, then I might as well hibernate like the rest of the animals in Barraine. More specifically, the rest of the animals whose homes haven't been turned into a fast food restaurant.

However, one of the benefits of Barraine is its close proximity to my parent's house in Countryhaven. Nick and I visit Countryhaven often. Last weekend in particular, I watched as Nick voluntarily assembled my mom's huge Christmas tree. As Nick was lying on his back underneath the 12-foot tree, my mom took her chance to express something quite exciting to her. I catch the gleam in her eye,

"I bet you'll be getting a ring for Christmas this year." Her eyebrows go up in that way like she knows something ahead of everyone else.

I'm sipping apple cider and vodka in a wine glass with the glowing warm lights of my family home surrounding me. I decide to glow a little warmer as I pour another shot into my homemade apple cider. Hank Williams Junior's voice booms through the speakers and we all get up to dance and sing around the kitchen island. My parents taught my brother, sister and I through their example to never miss an opportunity for fun. Nick tells me he loves me. I catch my reflection in the mirror and a peculiar thought pops through my mind: does he love me or does he love what he sees? I catch my dad watching Nick and me dance. I'm not sure what he's thinking but I know it's something.

As the night wraps up we drive back to Nick's house in Pittsburgh in the very old neighborhood of Scenic Hill, which is, to put it politely, a dodgy area of the city. Old skinny little homes, lodged in between other old skinny little homes which you wouldn't be able to justify fixing up based on the direction the neighborhood has gone. Nick is ready to get out of here and live somewhere with neighbors that are at least a football field away.

We're cuddled under a fluffy blanket as a movie plays on his giant television, my head resting against his shoulder, my brain in an altered state from the vodka in my hand. The drinking habit is something I had curbed for a while but it's recently been picking back up again. I justify that The Hobbit in 3D seems like a good enough reason.

By 11, I'm spent. I kiss Nick goodnight and walk into the bedroom. As my eyelids close I reach for my phone to turn it off when I notice an email. I'm awakened immediately, adrenaline coursing through me.

From: Dex

(no subject)

"Call me."

Jolted back awake, I take in a quick breath of air. As my hand goes weak I set down my phone quietly. I don't want Nick to know he's contacted me.

I really thought this was over.

CHAPTER 2
DEX

The day crawls by because I know I won't be able to call Dex until after 3:00 p.m., the time that he wakes up. I take a late lunch at work and practically sprint to my car, then drive to the first deserted lot I see, finding that familiar name and hitting dial, my heart pounding the whole way into my throat.

That evening Nick, my cousin Claire and I head to a friend's bar. Live music and Sambuca shots and by night's end we are all back at my apartment in the city where Claire takes the couch and Nick and I head to the bedroom.

It's 3:00 a.m. before I get the nerve to bring it up to Nick.

"I spoke with Dex today."

Nick's normally jovial face shifts with his hair-trigger temper.

"He needs me to film again. Sometime this weekend preferably."

Silence. But not for long. If Claire was sleeping in the other room, there was no chance of that now.

"Morgan!" he screamed at me. "*Why* is it taking Dex so long to finish his movie?! Why doesn't he hire an actress to play your role? He knows you aren't one. It doesn't make any sense. It's as if he expects you to be on his call and bend to his whims."

"We've already filmed so much footage, Nick, that hiring an actress would be like starting from square one. He said that he needs me – that this movie is his life's work and that he needs me to complete my part."

"This is his way of keeping you in his life and I'm not comfortable knowing that. No, Morgan. I'm NOT okay with it!"

"Nick, look, this project is something I started before you and I got back together. I feel obligated to complete it."

"You don't owe him anything, Morgan! Why do you let this man be your dictator?"

I attempt a rebuttal but Nick's not listening to anything I have to say, at all. His voice grows louder and louder in an attempt to override mine, something I've experienced many times before. Two hours of back and forth and we reach no real solution. He's so shook up he almost leaves a couple times but I convince him to stay.

I'm not sure how to remedy this one. I feel that I actually have an obligation to both men. It would be much easier to put this all behind me and move on healthily with Nick. But something tells me that decision would meet with violent opposition from Dex on the other end.

The sun feels like heaven on my skin, the vodka feels like blurred perception running happily through my veins, and the music flowing through his Bose feels like confidence vibrating in my body.

At 1:00 p.m., lying together on his red wooden balcony hidden high above the trees, the perfect summer song comes on and inspires me to pour another drink. I grab his heavy crystal lowball glass, walk into his shiny kitchen, and top both of our drinks off with fresh lime, ice, soda water, and Grey Goose. The Grey Goose has taught me how to move seductively today, and I do so, through his home back out to the balcony where he's lying there, shirtless, waiting for me.

Summer is the best time of the year in Pittsburgh. And this summer I am spending sporadic time with Rich, otherwise known as Eligible and Unavailable Bachelor # 1. I knew from the very first time Rich and I kissed that something didn't line up. I felt something kind of flash that turned me around on the inside and let me know that this wasn't it. Instead of ending things and listening to that gut reaction, I waited torturously for his infrequent calls.

"Take your shirt off," he softly demands. I'm hesitant but had a feeling it would go here so I'm prepared with a bra that somehow creates an optical illusion that I am two sizes bigger than I actually am. Sweat is dripping down his face and he is rubbing coconut-scented oil on my body.

Rich owns one of the nicest clubs in the city, wears suits to his office, and walks with the strut of a businessman whose internal mantra is, "I own you. I own this city. I own everything." I sensed it on him as soon as I met him. Walking up to me at a private party, saying way less than he needed to, he had me dreaming of our first date way before he even uttered, "what would you like to drink?"

Rich has recently presented the idea that my beautiful blonde cousin Claire and I should move in with him. We're not sure, but we think there's a chance that he was actually serious. And 20% of my brain actually pondered the idea for a minute. I allowed that 20% to weigh out the options of living with a man I barely know or living in an apartment that my parents are footing the bill for.

Since the beginning of the year I've been working part time for a nonprofit in an attempt to find some personal fulfillment. My day-to-day interactions are meaningful but my pay, not so meaningful. I'm making $1,000 per month working three days per week.

Day drinking on the balcony leads to an early dinner. Walking through the grocery store I throw everything into my cart that may have the power to impress him. It'll only take one day's pay for the extravagance that I will bake, sauté, and blend for him. Money is literally no object when it comes to something as important as food. He needs to know I can cook. He's probably assessing these sorts of things right now as traits of potential long-term compatibility. And the most important ingredient in my cart, by far, is the mint for the mojitos. This dinner (like most of them) will be washed down with hard liquor. Without the alcohol there would be zero chance of a conversation and zippo connection about anything.

The one exception to this rule, our one point of connection, is the subtle unspoken truth that Rich and I are here to validate one another. He validates me with his status in the world and his deep bottomless pockets that wine and dine me. I validate him by serving as the much younger accessory on his sport-coated arm—the girl sitting beside him in *his* club, wearing a snug coral-colored dress, drinking a mango jalapeño margarita.

One Sunday morning, I jumped out of Rich's bed (miraculously hangover free) and headed to the guest bath. Washing my face with the Korres face wash left behind from the last girl, I found myself surprisingly excited that Rich would be gone most of the day. Unique to this particular relationship was the strange phenomenon of having plenty to talk about over the phone yet having nothing to converse about in person. I figured that if Rich was at work all day, we'd have more to talk about upon his return.

After his $5,000 suit and $100,000 sports car pull away, I charge straight to his oversized bottle of Grey Goose. Flirting with rock bottom is not a new thing for me. It is my way of going into denial. I see how far I can push it before things have no choice but to change.

At the bottom of drink two, while looking through a bookshelf of books, my phone rings. It's Dex. Just in the nick of time, as always.

"Hello." I take the call but I'm not completely sure why. He's known me for three years and I know by now that there's not much I can keep from him.

"What the hell are you doing?" he blurts through the phone.

I'm trying to hide my 1:00 pm buzz is what I'm doing. I'm also trying to hide the way my voice is changing as I begin to cry.

"I don't know what I'm doing!" I'm sitting on a red chair looking out at a neighborhood filled with fancy doctor people walking around.

Somehow picking up that I'm in another man's home Dex continues, "You don't *have* to do this Morgan. You don't *have* to date anyone. Don't act desperate. You're not in any rush. You've got a million options!"

"Come to Los Angeles," he proposes. "It would be nice to see each other and we can also do some filming."

That evening Rich takes me to dinner downtown. The meal is delicious and after four drinks we are able to have a conversation. But by that point, the bar is closing and it's time to go home.

I crawl into his bed solo. He is downstairs in the kitchen making garlic bread for himself. Between the smells of fabric softener and garlic, I should feel at home. But as I peek out from beneath the Egyptian cotton, I realize there's nothing homey about it. I've never felt so alone in my whole life.

I'm going to Los Angeles.

CHAPTER 4
LOS ANGELES

"How quickly can you get to the airport? The flight leaves at 5:00." Dex's words on the other end excite me beyond belief. He's flying me to L.A. under the condition that I film while I'm there.

I've got 20 minutes to pack and get out the door. No shower. No makeup. I don't care. I've been waiting a long time to get to California!

I touch down in LAX at 11:00 PM.

The second the pilot says go, I dial him. "Dex, I'm here!!" I can't contain my excitement. I haven't seen Dex in three months since he began living in a $13 million mansion in Beverly Hills.

My first order of business: cuddling. But not his, however. As it always seems to be with him, I have to wait for a good thing.

"Call a taxi and meet me at the club. Give the taxi driver the address that I text you. We are filming."

"I'm in sweats!! I've been on a plane all day!"

"Get dressed and meet me at the club."

I could hear in his tone the slight anger of, "don't test me." I know I agreed to work while I was here—I just didn't imagine it would happen so soon.

So in the airport bathroom I rip into my luggage and change into a short black dress I bought five years ago. I put makeup on in the dark backseat of a taxi and pull my hair up into the best version of a ponytail I can.

The taxi drops me off in a parking garage near the club. I wait on the curb for Dex to come meet me. I'm entertained and slightly frightened by a five-foot-tall man wearing a sequined red blazer walking with two six-foot-tall hazy-eyed supermodels on each arm.

After 30 minutes, Dex walks around the corner wearing fitted jeans and a blue button-up shirt. He looks surprisingly well put together except for the wildness in his eyes. They are darting around as if preparing for an unforeseen attack.

We hug each other briefly. I had hoped for much more of an embrace after the length of time we've been apart. Without exchanging more than two words, it already feels as if we are in a fight. Plus, there's a cameraman following him and he's strategizing a shot. He's in work mode which is my least favorite mode to see him in because I get zero attention.

He tells me to wait in a line in which every girl is dressed impeccably. I'm dressed in every insecurity I've ever had in my life. I'm missing some secret form of socialization that every person in Hollywood understands. Before I can figure it out, I'm being led into the VIP section of one of the most exclusive nightclubs in Los Angeles at midnight, sober and alone. This is my worst nightmare.

Dex is currently pursuing the path of a filmmaker. His keen mind and relentless ambition usually equates with making the seemingly impossible possible in whatever path he is on. His uncanny knack for understanding human nature allows him to predict what people will do and when they will do it. He describes it as being "three steps ahead of everyone."

So now he's setting his sights on where so many thousands have dreamed of conquering: Hollywood. And I happened to be the little girl running around Pittsburgh who caught his eye who somehow, someway, got cast in a film with Hollywood stars who had worked their whole lives to be household names.

When I first met him, I didn't know if I could believe that he was really working in the film industry. I also didn't know if I liked him. But as time went on, my opinion was being swayed in his favor. For this reason, he never missed an opportunity to tell me that I was shallow. After all, he'd say, "You wouldn't fuck me until you realized that I'm also dating supermodels."

Dex's six-foot body was not particularly defined by any sort of muscular definition. In his opinion, a man who cared too much about his appearance didn't have much going on in his personality. So Dex didn't try. He avoided mirrors, picked his outfits from a pile of unwashed T-shirts on his bedroom floor and combed his thick hair never. He maintained beautifully soft hands and long delicate fingers, never having done any sort of physical labor in his life aside from typing on his keyboard and clicking his mouse.

Our first date had begun at a nice restaurant in Shadyside and ended at a strip club on the outskirts of the city at 4 a.m., my head lying in his lap on the cab ride home and the city swirling around in a circle as I peered out the window. I had just turned 25 and I was a lost little girl. So much so that when we got home, I chose to walk into his dark bedroom even though everything in my body screamed a resounding "No!" I wanted to be loved so badly, especially by someone like him. So I took his next call and then his next and ended up in his condo, each time trying to invent persuasive enough reasons why I had to go home before it was time to go to bed. How I could maintain the attention of a "filmmaker" without having to do something—that didn't feel right to me. Eventually I crowded out my instinct and convinced myself that it *did* feel right. The exciting opportunities popping up around him because of his movie helped enhance my attraction to him.

As much as Dex repulsed me, he also intrigued me. His mind excited me and I loved my ability to go there with him. He was a gifted communicator, the most persuasive person to walk planet earth, and a genius. We laughed a lot and we talked on a much different level

than I ever had. Our average phone conversation lasted four hours. We spoke more on the phone than we ever saw each other in person. After 20 minutes of dictation that could not have been more eloquently communicated by the president himself, he'd pause.
"Are you listening?"
"Yes I'm listening."
"Then repeat back to me in your own words what I've just explained."

His voice held a deepness and authoritative energy that could be felt behind his words. No "ums" or "I don't knows." No pauses or breaks. His speech was filled with meaning and purpose. Something about him made me want to keep listening. He took on the role of a mentor and showed me his way of navigating the world. Because of him I started to see opportunity where I had never seen it. He taught me that if there was something that I really wanted, I could go get it. He taught me how to think bigger, MUCH bigger.

I occasionally handed him the reins to my life, where sometimes, I trusted him more than I trusted myself to make decisions. I listened to his advice because I didn't know if anyone else knew how to see the world the way he did. It seemed he was in on some sort of secret knowledge. He was also completely and utterly confident in his wisdom which made him that much more convincing. And based on what I was watching him do in the world, I'd never met anyone else who was so keenly able to make things happen.

Often he gave really good, really firm advice. For example, after months of prodding me on what he perceived was a gluten intolerance, I went gluten free. That decision completely changed my life. After months of prodding me to cut back on alcohol, *that* decision completely changed my life. After years of prodding me to stop using men for their status, I finally heard what he was saying. It would take another two years before that decision would completely change my life. And so on and so on and so on. All the positive life changes were undeniable. But there was one very huge elephant in the room that was impossible to miss: I was handing over the reins of my life (voluntarily) to someone other than myself.

As for us, he mentored me towards his vision of an ideal relationship. But it always seemed that I could never quite get to the level the teacher was looking for so that he could step out of the role of the teacher.

He specified right from the first date, "I don't want to get married or have children." *We* all knew that from the beginning. His phone was never on, his shoes never tied, and his car was always filthy and filled with glass water bottles. But he had women left, right and center and we were all fairly aware that there were probably others. In fact, he'd openly talk about it. He didn't buy us things—that wasn't the attraction. He didn't take us to fancy dinners. He didn't believe in that. Dex had something else that drew us all in.

The Pattern

I began to love the man but it was torture. He seemed to only come home to Pittsburgh right when I had just gotten over him. Then he would stay just long enough to hook my heart again and make me doubt the already questionable relationship I was pursuing at the time.

We had a pattern. When his parents (who had no idea of my existence for three years) left town, we'd go to their mansion in the country. We'd hold each other for 12 hours, only separating long enough to eat a meal. Then we'd cling right back on for another 12 hours.

Things would appear happy and peaceful and, just like that, we were in the whirlwind again. I'm experiencing moments of such brief happiness that, in the shower, I'm drawing hearts with the steam. Then I'm adding a little check mark beside it. As I got ready, he would tell me to skip the makeup because he liked me better without it. Then he'd drive us through Pittsburgh to streets and places I had never seen. We'd glide through Squirrel Hill where he'd say he was looking to buy a house. I wondered if someday, maybe I'd be living in it. My excitement would start to build. But just as I started to curl into the idea, he'd leave. Back to New York or Los Angeles. More work and a promise that he'd be back much sooner than he ever actually was. Back to the 4:00 a.m. calls that if I didn't notice my phone lighting up the first time, he'd call four more times. Back to listening so closely to his words for even the slightest clues of when he would *actually* be coming home. And back to being stopped dead in my tracks in the middle of the Whole Foods soap aisle when I smelled the lavender scented soap that his mother had in her kitchen. Right in the middle of aisle 11, dead in my tracks, with a broken heart.

When he *was* at home in Pittsburgh, long days were spent in his bed together. I began to turn nocturnal like him. When my friends and family couldn't reach me until 5:00 p.m., it was a dead giveaway that I was with Dex. And the people closest to me bit their tongues most of the time.

His first stop of the day was always Whole Foods. He'd grab a salad and some form of meat or fish which would be cooked on a George Foreman with years of grime stacked on its plates. I would scrub it in the bathtub because his kitchen sink was always full of dishes and something rotting.

Then we would head back to his condo to watch a movie that we'd criticize the whole time unless it was really "good," which was a rarity. The only two films that checked out were *Labyrinth* and a film where a man goes to live with grizzly bears and eventually gets eaten by them. The latter freaked me out for weeks. Or we'd

watch Beavis and Butthead which was *always* really
entertaining due to "Mike Judge's ability to represent his
personalized anger towards other humans within the
confines of a cartoon," or so we both agreed. At 2:00
a.m. I'd go to bed while he sat on his Mac with 20 open
Safari tabs, on a mission. I was never quite sure if I was
part of that mission or just a passerby to stimulate his
perpetual brain activity. At 4:00 a.m. he would come to
bed and we'd go into the "brain zone" where we'd talk
with such conviction you'd have thought we had figured
out the world's problems.

The urgency of this conviction fueled his brain.
Being around him took intense focus. So when it was
time to shut down, he'd shut down and sleep for 12
hours. Sometimes his brain wouldn't shut down
completely, but instead, it would figure out solutions
while he was dreaming. This is what he told me. In his
pitch black room, on a hill overlooking the city, a
mastermind think tank was taking place. Sometimes
with me in his arms.

But also, always, a little anger for me, for us,
simmered beneath the surface. He was condescending
and suppressive. He said I needed to be knocked down
a bit, so I could understand reality, before I could be
built back up. And then he would ask me not to get
angry. If I got angry he said he would take me home and
not speak to me for months. Even with all of his

ultimatums and an anger management class, I could never hold it in for long.

We fueled something in each other that was destructive and almost impossible to stifle. I'd scream, "What if I'm spending the prime years of my life with a man that never ends up making a commitment to me?"

"That's possible…" he'd say, "but you don't have the tools to be in a healthy relationship right now anyway." And of course, if he said it, it must be true.

That would stew within me for a couple days. Then he'd question my motives about some course of action I was taking, calling them impure, and that would be the icing. POP. I'd snap, and his Xbox controller goes flying across the room. He's screaming. I threaten to stab him with a huge ornamental wooden fork lying in the middle of his cluttered hallway. He holds my suitcase hostage during the time period that I really need it when my brother is letting me stay on his couch. These eruptions that just wouldn't be stifled.

<u>The Pattern Broken Down</u>:

1. I'd misbehave in some way like the above.

2. Dex: "We can't talk for a while. Maybe never again."

3. For three days I'd be very sad. I'd sulk around. I'd beat myself up for screwing things up. Breakup songs are playing in my Jeep.

4. Day 4: The magic happens. I begin feeling lighter. Almost better.

5. Day 7: I'm on with my life. Friends and family are noticing how much happier I appear.

6. Day 8: My phone rings. Dex very lovingly: "I'm calling to check on you. Someday you'll understand how much I love you. You'll understand why I do what I do. I need to have enough respect for myself not to be around someone who treats me poorly."

7. "I'm so sorry Dex. I love you."

8. Back in the whirlwind.

There was a reason I felt relieved when Dex and I weren't talking: I was always two inches from an anxiety attack when we were! Scared to do something wrong. Scared to endure another breakup with him for the mistakes that I would make. Scared to find out that maybe I was a bad person who may never be able to get it together. Scared to hurt him again. And since I enrolled myself in life training with him, I allowed for his strict approach to happiness and success. But characteristically, I was always able to find something wrong with myself. He'd say, "Forgive yourself." Like those words were that simple to put into action. But I didn't know how. I wanted to keep beating myself up. I wanted to assume that there was some unforgivable flaw hiding around the next bend. I wanted to punish myself for being bad. I wanted to uncover every single bad thing within so I could grow. I thoroughly beat myself up in the process. Even when Dex was pointing out the light, I almost always saw the dark.

But yet, we also kind of knew there was something powerful going on between us. Once in a while, hidden there, right before falling asleep in each other's arms, was love. The pure type of love that surpassed all of the human drama. The intensity of this love made everything so much more confusing. The only part that we really had nailed was the times when we were sleeping.

Listening to his breath go in and out. Realizing I was holding mine. These moments that we had 1/20th of the time were enough. Enough to keep going, enough to suffer through the volatility, and enough to think we just might get it right. In the deepest trenches with him I fought for air, for light, for life—stimulated by the mere fact that we may not survive.

<u>Los Angeles</u>

He's hosting a pool party with guests walking around that I've seen on television. I'm trying to hide in the house where the caterers and bartenders are working. I'd rather wait for this to pass safely as to not encounter any awkward interactions with the L.A. social scene. This is not his wish, however. He is demanding, not asking, that I join the party. Tears of insecurity are streaming down my face as we stand in his marble-laden master bath together. He points the camera towards my face. "You are so beautiful Morgan, look at you." I look in the mirror.

I don't even think it matters at the moment if I'm beautiful or not. I look out the window to a group of people who have this thing down in the middle of a world I couldn't have prepared for if I tried. I'm terrified.

My worst nightmare continued: Being set free alone in my bathing suit, to introduce myself and socialize among the most intimidating people I've ever seen.

The L.A. week continues on like this. Somehow, I start to slightly enjoy the social interactions once I realize that the people aren't as scary as I thought. Dex senses this and takes me to sit in on a meeting with a producer on a road called Melrose. There are framed posters of movies all over his red velvet walls. Dex doesn't prep me at all for this meeting, which is good. I don't really want to know how important this guy is until I'm out of here. I'm wearing a black sundress I've owned for ten years and a pair of silver sandals. My legs are crossed. And I try not to make any movements that will draw attention to me. Once the meeting is done, Dex tells me I did a good job.

During a rare block of free time, when I had Dex to myself, we held each other in the cabana. We did what we did well together: sleep for long periods of time. I awoke in a daze to the sparkling backdrop of L.A. and a deep, deep lonely feeling. I asked out loud. "Will I ever be able to be as close to someone as we are right now? Will I be able to love someone so much again?"

He didn't blink and didn't pause. "Yes."

The certainty in his voice felt like a dagger to my chest.

The night before I left L.A. we lay in bed, my heart aching because I was leaving and didn't know what was next for us. He ventured, "maybe you can come back and live here." My heart lifted. Then a silence where we both already knew the answer.

"No," we said in unison. Not yet.

I arrive back in Pittsburgh where the summer is still warm. I'm lying on my parents' back porch with a view of nothing but hilly green fields and big beautiful pines. No pool parties, no Bentleys, no models, no flashing lights. Dex's call is the only sound that breaks the silence. I pick up the phone but decide to set it back down. I close my eyes and the memory of a previous conversation flashes through my head:

"I want you to know that if you are sweet, you get everything you want. You just can't keep your shit together long enough. If you could keep it together, I'd want you living with me."

CHAPTER 5
AUGUST 2013

After returning from L.A., I was ready to jump off the three-year roller coaster ride with Dex. Los Angeles was exciting, California was amazing, but I could not wait any longer for a relationship that was always just out of reach.

I needed to figure out my next step in life instead of my next step with a man. I wanted to start a new career. I wanted to move somewhere warm. The route to both of those things looked like schooling as a naturopathic doctor, something I had always been interested in.

In order to gain insight and guidance, I began contacting every doctor I knew. It all happened pretty quickly. It started with a text to a man who years before had experienced with me a wild and dramatically passionate relationship: Nick. Through text we decided it may be a little easier to speak on the phone. Once on the phone, we thought it may be a little easier to speak in person. Once in person, we thought it may be a little easier to live together. Within two weeks, I had gone from searching for my life path to being in a full-blown relationship.

When I saw Nick walking through the garage door of that Lawrenceville bar, I saw something I had been waiting a long time to see. He walked like a man that made no apology for his existence. I noticed his tan skin and immediately liked it.

After a familiar hug, we sat down together at a seat with a view of Butler Street. Then I start talking about my idea for the future which we both kind of know is about to change.

"There's a school in Southern California that looks nice. It's definitely my top choice for location."

He offers his advice until I realize that I'm not really interested in figuring this out right now.

"What would you like to drink?" His white teeth were beaming in an upturned smile, his eyes sparkling a turquoise blue.

"I'll have the same as you. "

He walks back with a frosty glass of Ketel One, soda water, and a huge slice of orange. He squeezes the juice of the orange into my drink. I take a big sip of exhilaration. His drink choice is perfect.

The night takes on its own surprising rhythm. Drink one and the conversation flows. Drink two, and there's an obvious electricity in the air. Drink three, there's an excitement in my bones. At midnight he throws his card down on the wooden bar—his hand on my hip as he signs his name. Ketel One, a handsome doctor, and my whole life has changed.

December 2013

Four Months Later

One very snowy day, I watched as we loaded my belongings out of my 45th Street Lawrenceville apartment. Alone in this apartment I had lived for three years. Now, Nick is helping me leave. Apartment #107 held me close, rocked me to sleep, and relished with me in my most adventurous years. These walls felt the pangs of loneliness, the hope of new love, the careless freedom and laughter with friends old and new. In this tiny kitchen I chopped my own vegetables and fed my body from the money I had earned myself. In this bedroom I dreamt of places unknown so glorious and beautiful that I longed to see more. In this living room I sat my body in meditation and asked to know God. Within these walls I found out who I was and I found out who I wasn't.

Walking around my beloved space one more time, the pain of nostalgia gripped at my chest. Nick's head tilted sideways when I asked that he give me a minute alone here. He didn't quite understand why I had to say goodbye. He didn't quite understand that a little girl became a woman within these walls.

I move into Nick's house in Scenic Hill. I let out a long breath that I didn't know I was holding. The whole experience was bittersweet, after all. I could finally stop looking for a man. I had spent three years in this apartment desperately trying to do just that.

CHAPTER 6
THREE YEARS EARLIER

When I got my first real job, I moved into apartment #107 where I lived on my own in a city for the first time. Free, independent and single all at once and I was ready to break some rules. Not wasting any time, the first thing I did was fall in love with a man 25 years older than me.

I spent a good year longing for him. I talked to everyone I knew. Some said age didn't matter. Some said, you're crazy. I never quite got an answer. What I did get was a constant anxious feeling in my chest and the deep desire of wanting to be wanted.

Before I met him, I saw him first. He was standing on the sidewalk in Lawrenceville, a white shirt perfectly framing him, a confident conviction rooting his stoic body to the earth. In a split second I felt the fire of passion ignite my entire being.

We were both wearing sunglasses as we caught a quick glance of each other. I wished so badly to have seen his eyes. I wished so badly that he could've seen mine. Then he would've seen the way I came to life when I saw him. As the light turned green, I reluctantly put my foot on the gas, and just like that, the moment was gone. But not really.

I dialed my mom. "If there are men that look like that in this city, I am excited to be single. "

Two days later, mystery sidewalk man confidently approaches me in a quiet bar. I turn down his offer for a drink but I entertain the conversation briefly. He hypothesized I was "just coming out of a relationship or tired of being hit on so much." He explained that he didn't know why but he *had* to talk to me. His name is Cash and he, too, lives in Lawrenceville a short 11 blocks away.

Cash is my idea of handsome. And his age has only enhanced his looks. It's as if each year has taken his best features and made them even better. His sculpted cheekbones, his strong shoulders, his deep voice. Sometimes I felt like a naïve country girl in his presence. But Cash didn't seem to mind. Nothing seemed to bother the man who, when he finds out you've scraped your finger, draws it to his lips. I don't know the color of his eyes because that's not what I notice. What I notice is what I feel. What I feel is the primal longing *behind* his eyes. And that primal longing is directed at me.

The next day, the day I turned 25, we went on our first date. He took my hand as I got out of the low, red leather seat of his car. He still hadn't told me his age yet but I knew, oh I knew, I was on the brink of something dangerous. The feeling of his hand on mine felt forbidden and took my breath away. He wasn't afraid like I was and I liked it. He held the door as we walked into a bar covered with red velvet walls. He ordered his favorite vodka for us and said it was the best. Then, without saying anything, he asked me to bare my soul. Then he listened. He tilted his head and gazed at me like he'd never seen a woman, like he'd never seen anything beautiful, like he was experiencing both for the first time, right there. As I opened up about something I loved, mid-sentence I felt him lean in, his lips on mine. Everything stopped. The world. My voice. Except my heart felt a new sensation: the longing for a man twice my age who knew how to move about the world and make me feel like a woman, not a girl.

The desire for powerful men was a new experience for me and it would quickly become my downfall. I didn't know a man like Cash could be putty in my hands. I came from Countryhaven, Pennsylvania after all. How could such a powerful man be interested in me?

It seemed that everything I did was amazing to him. When he finally did admit his age, 49, I didn't blink. I wasn't attached yet. I told him I would continue to see other people and that the age gap probably wouldn't work, but we could keep seeing each other as long as it did.

But something was happening. As "innocent" as I thought it was to leave one of my match.com dates and run to his apartment, I was totally and completely wrong.

"How was your date," he asked in his deep calm voice once I arrived at his apartment.

"I was thinking about *you*," I would say, wondering if he could sense my confusion.

Next thing I know he's got me on his bed and he's got NO shame in the way he shows his attraction. There's an electricity, a magnetism and fire kindling between us. Our bodies feel pulled to one another. It takes every ounce of my will power to walk out of his apartment and not let this go further than I'm ready for. Every ounce. When I pull into my parking lot five minutes later I receive a phone call. He's talking in almost a whisper with the vibrancy and quickness of an excited child,

"Morgan, I didn't know I could feel this way again. It's amazing."

And I listen with a jumpy little tickle in my stomach. As I crawl into my bed, a huge smile forms on my face. Even though I know that this situation makes no sense, I'm feeling it, too.

I ate up every word that came out of his mouth. I clung to them as if he was letting me in on the secret to my own femininity. He kept telling me, "You have no idea how powerful you are," and I was actually starting to believe him. Anything I wore, he liked. Any way I did my hair, he grabbed. Anything I said, he was interested in. He started saying, "I love everything about you." And after a while it began to catch, because when I was around him, I began to see myself in a new way: as beautiful, as intelligent.

I was so comfortable and secure that it felt like very little risk to finally stay with him. So on Halloween evening, a sparkly, bright-eyed disco queen found a home in his fluffy white California King. I didn't expect things to change. But they did. For both of us.

I knew something was different the next morning. He didn't rush me out of his house or anything—the signs weren't that evident. He took me to breakfast. We drank a Bloody Mary. He spoke to me the same way. But when the time came to get out of his car outside of my apartment, I felt a new and uncomfortable feeling.

"I'm going to miss you," I said, the words almost pouring from my mouth. As soon as they were spoken, I knew that they didn't fit. I sensed the uncomfortableness in the little black sports car that all of a sudden seemed too small for two. As soon as I walked into my apartment, alone, my heart plummeted into the deep, deep water of regret.

The heaviness came from this: I glimpsed what I believed to be my own power in his eyes, and I didn't know how to retrieve it without him.

His texts became less frequent, his phone calls nonexistent. My heart ached as I felt him distancing himself from the passion and desperation that ensued from our 25-year age gap. He wasn't gone completely, however—no. We still saw each other periodically, me holding my breath until he showed up again. One time in particular, after a little coaxing from me, he showed up on an icy cold evening. He walked up to the top of 45th Street. Then he called. It had been three weeks since I'd seen him.

I walk to the door.

I see his breath before I see him.

Then like every good piece of art, there he is.

He's holding the space of quiet contentment of a man who needed nothing.

A barely existent smile only evidenced by his eyes. Of a secret he only knew.

Holding the secret of pain, of exhaustion, and of lust. I lived for it. And I waited for it.

He stood in the entryway of my apartment leaning on the brick wall, staring into the distance. If I had never come to that door, it seemed that he may have never known the difference. He may have kept staring off into the night sky, the steam from his breath rising in the 18-degree air. Maybe the memory of the hopeful 25-year-old woman running down the hall to greet him

36

would disappear just as quickly as his warm breath in the frigid air.

"It's raining." he says. I already know as the water from his scarf touches my neck.

He follows me into my apartment. There's a sitcom on my television. I've never watched the show in my life but I flicked it on because it seemed neutral enough so he couldn't guess that I actually wasn't watching television at all. I had been actually changing and then changing again, then putting on perfume and reassessing my makeup in the mirror a million times.

The lighting is soft. My Himalayan salt lamp is lit, casting a soft orange glow through my tiny living room.

"Let's go to dinner," he says, and everything in my body lifts with excitement. And he gets me to our restaurant with the copper backdrop and dark hardwood floors and makes me believe that he missed me, too. That the urgency that I feel is the urgency that he feels too. That the three-week gap was too tortuous and it would never happen again. I'm hearing EVERY SINGLE THING that I've been wanting to hear.

I float through dinner. He's feeding me quail eggs off of a skewer dipped in ponzu butter.

The bartender approaches, "Would you like another drink?"

No.

Up to his top floor loft and he's got me pinned against the brick. I forget that he hasn't called, he hasn't texted, he hasn't cared—right now his body is promising me that he does. So I go with it because more than anything else I want to feel like that goddess again that I see when he's looking at me.

I only need a small glimmer of hope to keep on. That hope comes with the toothbrush he's still keeping for me in his bathroom, the memory from that very first night forever embedded in my mind. My head tilted back in laughter as he carried me from his bed to that toothbrush when I told him I was too tired to walk. That toothbrush reminds me of his enthusiasm for this relationship as it once was.

He stood with me in the moonlight and held me with a promise I swear I could feel. But the promise may just have been my own because there came a point when he didn't show up very often anymore. Then, eventually, he didn't show up at all.

I wondered if everything I ever said to him sounded like a child. I just wanted him to admire me. I just wanted him to love me. I just wanted to feel intelligent. "Love me! Love me! Please God love me!" On my hands and knees. A little child begging for acceptance. He knew something that I didn't want to admit. I was too addicted to the relationship to see the situation clearly.

I wrote him a letter. I said sorry. I said thank you. I said I love you without saying I love you. I pretended that I was okay with parting because it was the most rational thing to do. I pretended that parting had been *my* decision.

He responded a few days later. He offered reassurance of his feelings. He talked about seeing my soul for what it is. He expressed that the one giant obstacle (age difference) didn't seem to exist when we were together. He urged me not to get caught up with men who try to impress me with the wrong things. He told me to hold out for real happiness. That he knew it was there for me. He thanked me for every moment I gave him.

And when it was all said and done,

"Every moment was worth it. "

-Cash

I read the letter to my mom. She said, "It sounded like that man loved you, Morgan." That made me want him even more.

As the weeks went by without any sort of contact from him, I found that it didn't matter whether he loved me or not. It wasn't enough to bring him back.

CHAPTER 7
MY PLAN SEEMED TO BE WORKING

Cash and I were done but that didn't stop me from looking around every corner for him for a year. Driving around Lawrenceville, Taylor Swift's "Speak Now" album became my anthem and therapy. I prayed that maybe he'd step out of a coffee shop as I was walking by. I knew he was always within blocks of me. I knew we were always within one coincidental meeting away from a reconciliation. I could feel him, but I couldn't do anything about it.

One mysteriously windy Sunday, I walked down Butler Street. The leaves spinning in a tornado on the ground, rustling to a chaotic rhythm. Something unsettling in the air. Something unsettled inside of me. Watching it all from behind, a faceless man and a faceless woman step out onto Butler Street. I struggle to get closer. Could it be? Is it him? The wind whips through the trees, plastic bags flying through the streets, so many people blocking the view, enjoying an irregularly sunny day, walking so slowly. I just need to see. I just need to know. Closer. Closer. I watch the pair make a left onto 40th and disappear into a building. Cash's building. Before I can blink, they are gone. And just like that, my hope for Cash is, too.

From here, my mid-twenties turned into a waiting game. I had to let go of Cash but that didn't stop the waiting. Waiting on a text from a man. Waiting on an action from a man. Waiting on a man. Period. And there were many. It was the best and the worst time of my life all at once.

Pittsburgh was my refuge, though. If I could wrap my arms around it and hug this city, I would. Because that city forgave me so many times and helped brush the dirt off my knees. Pittsburgh was a microcosm of a world much bigger, a world I imagined in which I was able to make mistakes and still be lifted back onto my feet.

When I wasn't making vodka gummy bears, I took walks alone. So many freakin' times. Down the Lawrenceville streets and alleys and hidden places I walked. To Bloomfield and to the river. I walked everywhere I could in order to get my mind off of whatever man I was waiting on. And I started to see beauty in the areas that at first did not seem beautiful. In the old dilapidated houses. In the torn-up cobblestone streets. I walked away to temporarily escape the life I was leading. A life that didn't really line up with who I was but offered me excitement if nothing else.

I experienced only brief moments of deep connection to myself when I allowed—journaling my feelings, meditating, and attending a spiritual church where the people there had so much love in their hearts that you feel like crying when you hug them. In my soul, I longed so deeply for a man who would enjoy delving into the deeper things with me. My interests had always been in the magic of life and in the connection to something bigger, but most of the time, alcohol covered up and filled in any chance of self that was trying to come through. I used alcohol for two completely opposite purposes: to discover myself and to suppress myself. Alcohol was my way to feel and not feel all at once.

Despite my higher aspirations, I lived under a definite theme of men who were all uniquely alike. Dating men who are actively using their phone to Facebook for the entirety of dinner. *Then*, taking trips with these *same* men in which I keep a freshly poured drink in my hand for 12 hours to avoid the discomfort of the situation I put myself in. Big houses on lakes with boats and fast cars. They all still suck when you're lying to yourself.

Dating men with trust funds filled with old money, who party every single night of the week, and who show up with two other women to an event he invited *me* to. Dating men who talk about going on vacations to St. Martin together and who talk about coming home to meet my family only to pull the "slow fade"* once they get what they want.

They always, always, always put their best foot forward and aggressively pursued for two weeks. Then after two weeks (my average obligatory breaking point

---

* *My definition of the "slow fade": gradually reducing communication and depth of text responses in an attempt to elusively slip out of a relationship without ever having to feel bad about hurting someone's feelings by telling the truth. Real life example: A period of time went by when he'd only contact me at midnight or later, tell me how drunk he was and then ask if I was out, too. Then it would be my responsibility to get into a cab and meet him in an entirely opposite part of the city from where I was currently socializing. No more dinners. No more movies. Unless of course the occasional circumstance in which his luck had probably run dry in the bars along the South Side. Then once in a while I'd get a text like, "Happy Easter!" or even more surprising, "Happy Valentine's Day!"*

which I usually based on the amount of money they had invested on dates) they always, always, always changed their minds.

My cousin Claire and I would call each other daily. "What do you think he meant by, 'I'm so hungover?' Should I respond?"

"No, I would make him wait," Claire's voice as adamant about her philosophy as one could be.

Nice men with Honda Civics, kind eyes, beautiful faces, and good manners made their rounds, too. They seemed a little too boring once they started liking me a little too much. If they were ready for a relationship, I was ready to say "see ya!"

So I got exactly what excited me: a man who knew how to make money, walk with the arrogance of having slept with a million girls, and pick the right suit for his preferably tall body. I wanted to feel like I was with the most powerful man in the room, without compromise. It made me feel important and it made me feel like I was someone in Pittsburgh, too.

My subconscious plan seemed to work. I was put in magazines, recognized for my accomplished career and work within the community. I got to know as many people as I could from the band members, bartenders, bar backs, managers, owners, waitresses, young people, old people, athletes, friends of friends. Everywhere I went was an exciting opportunity to grow my network.

Expensive drinks were poured for me most nights as well as the occasional afternoon binge on a nice boat. I had an invite anywhere I wanted and I took it. I knew everyone and if I didn't know them, I knew how to connect to them.

As time went by the same pattern continued. He (a.k.a. unattainable, noncommittal man) took me somewhere fancy. I took him somewhere fancy. He introduced me to someone fancy. I introduced him to someone fancy. The more money they were willing to dish out on a date, the more potential I saw in a relationship. The really ironic part about the whole thing was for the amount of effort I put into capturing one of these men, it never happened. None of it ever materialized. One reason is because deep down, men don't want something fake. The other reason was that deep down, neither did I.

Chapter 8
The Breakdown

Only so much of this could be endured. I could not go anywhere or do anything in the social scene that I hadn't already done. I had tried every type of food at every pretty restaurant. I had worn every tight jean, high boot combo I could think of. What was once so exciting really lost its luster when I realized it was all the same. After two solid years of partying it was not so fun anymore.

So I began taking long walks through the graveyard and sleeping with a pillow behind my back, pretending that someone was holding me. I would go to the movie *Jane Eyre* alone and then cry in my car, thinking about the trees that were dead and wilting from the cold rain. I spent a majority of my free time in the Lawrenceville library which became my refuge and place of hope amidst all the confusion.

Then, I did the unthinkable and quit my "dream job" in the city. This action marked the beginning of the people around me starting to believe I may have a mental illness. No one could wrap their brain around how I could leave a corporate job in which I made my own hours and had full access to the major sports and entertainment venues throughout the city. I shattered a lot of dreams that day, but not my own. I found out quickly that the psychic all of the women in my family had been consulting, who predicted I would marry a professional athlete, was dead wrong.

I moved back home to the country, to my childhood room. I avoided people in Countryhaven as to not have to explain why the girl they had seen on the front page of their newspaper was now circling the drain back in her hometown. Get-togethers with old college friends became uncomfortable. Their lives seemed so stable and consistent. Mine was ever-changing.

So I tucked myself into my room and began spending long hours reading my books about spirituality and focusing on my meditation practice. My family tried to get me out of my bedroom but I usually replied with, "No, I am completely satisfied with what I am doing here." I spent a long winter in solitude, introspection and rest. I spent a long winter sober. The first time in 10 years.

Childhood memories began flooding back. I remembered walking through the forest with my father and grandfather, each one of their strides equaling two of my own. My father gazing back at me noticing my attempt to keep up. "Look ahead and the rest will come into view," he had said. Back through the front door of our warm home, the overwhelming smells of stew and fresh pie awaited us, my mother and grandmother moving about the kitchen. I was only about eight when I sat in front of a crackling fire and uncovered the mysteries of life. Where had all the clarity gone? Where was this little girl now?

Dex was there during this time of solitude, trying to help me pick up my quarter-life crisis pieces. He'd say, "You have no problems. The saddest thing in the world is wasted potential. Now get out there and go figure out what you want for your life."

But I had no idea what I wanted for my life. So he had to basically force me out of my bed to shadow the people with careers I thought I may enjoy. He urged me to figure out a career path that I would love. Slowly but surely I began coming around. I began propping myself up on the couch with my brother's mini red laptop. I researched. I read. I tried to figure myself out. I saw one trend: Kids. I liked kids. I wanted to be around them. I always had. So I looked for jobs that would allow me to do this. I contacted CEOs from around the country in companies that served kids. If the job was in New York, or Chicago or wherever, I would be willing to go. I sent out hundreds of emails. For every hundred, I got two responses. For every two responses, I got one phone call. "One response could change your entire life," Dex would say. So I kept going, the bigger the better. And for some reason, I had no shame or problem in hearing "No."

Brainwashed, however, from growing up in a society that believes a certain way, I still interviewed for the occasional 9-5, or even more obnoxious 8:30-5:00 office job that I had little interest in. The severity of receiving such an offer could have been fatal. I saw the paycheck but not the 40 hours of hell within a confined space it would take to get it. An offer, quite simply, would have been a death sentence to me. Luckily, the managers interviewing me picked up that I was noncommittal and never hired me. Training myself to do something I hated every day for money went against every fiber of my being. Plus, I knew in my heart that doing something I loved would eventually pay off far, far greater than any of these jobs.

CHAPTER 9
TRANSITION

All my work began to pay off when I found an organization in Pittsburgh that I believed in. I began volunteering for a nonprofit that worked with financially challenged children. I was interacting one on one with kids and I found a purpose. So when they offered me a job for three days a week at $1,000 a month, I took it.

All was well and good for about a year. Then the point came when I had learned just about all I had wanted to learn at the nonprofit. That's when the universe dealt me a new deck of cards: Nick came back into my life.

I left my job. I left my apartment. And I started a life with him at the new office he was opening in Barraine.

Barraine Strip Mall

In my hand I hold a paintbrush covered in Cypress Green. The walls of the sterile office space are becoming tranquil Zen with each brush stroke. Today Nick was handed the keys to his brand-new office in Barraine. His dream of having his own space has become a reality and we are all here, family and friends, to create his vision.

I will be working full time with Nick to build his practice and to create a holistic health center for the people of Barraine. Having a center like this is something I've thought a lot about in my life. Ordering an inventory of vitamins and natural products to stock the shelves, I get to put the years of studying holistic healing into practice.

Nick is promising me not only creative freedom but a location in which I can start health counseling once I've graduated from nutrition school. Nick was the main encourager of me going back to school so I will have a little more validation in this field and within his practice.

He's got his arm around my shoulder and his dad is snapping a picture. Paint is covering my yoga pants but none of that matters. We are happy and excited and hopeful.

I walk around the office with a burning piece of sage when the mailman walks through the door. He's carrying a huge plant. He asks us to sign as he places a giant peace lily on the floor.

"Who's it from, Morgan?"

"I'm trying to find the...oh here it is!" I pick up the card with a confused look on my face.

"What is it?" his face is concerned and rightfully so.

"This plant is from Nancy, John and Bob. Do you know a Nancy, John and Bob? I don't."

His voice is a little more urgent now, "No. Flip the card over…"

I do as instructed and read the message aloud: "We are so sorry for your loss. Sending love and sympathy to you during this time."

"What is this about Nick? This plant was supposed to go to a funeral not to our office!"

I tried to conceal from him how I was feeling inside. Like this was a kind of sign, that there *was* a death here, but I couldn't figure out who, or what it was. Or would be.

I keep searching the plant frantically and find another card stapled to the other side:

To: Morgan and Nick

"Congratulations on your new business venture! Best of luck to you both!

-Mom, Dad, Aunt J & Uncle E"

I put the card down and stand back up, slightly off balance, my stomach turning.

Shrugging and trying to hide just how freaked out I am, I look at Nick.

"The florist must have made a mistake. "

I know it must've been a big step for my dad to send the flowers because last week he sat me down for a serious conversation. He sat at the head of the table with a look on his face I'd never seen before.

"Morgan, can I talk to you for a minute?"

"Yes." I sit down at the other end of our family table.

He takes his glasses off and begins to rub his eyes. I see his jawbone begin to pulse as he clenches his teeth. I know something uncomfortable is coming because my dad has never asked me to sit down for a solo serious conversation in my life.

"Do you know what you are doing getting back together with Nick? From what you said about the relationship the first time, you said he was trying to control you. Plus, the way he took the breakup…"

Nick had gone through a rough time after we broke up three years ago, rougher than I even knew. He stayed on his parents' couch for I don't know how long mending his heart. I think he kind of assumed that we would get back together. I had other plans, though, which began when Cash popped in and enlivened my view on life.

"Dad, I've changed. I've become so much more mature. I made it really hard on him the first time we dated."

"I hear you talking about how you've changed but what about him?"

Boom. Well I hadn't thought about that. I had just assumed that most of our original issues came from me. From my continued communication with other men and my inability to control my anger because of alcohol.

"It seems like he's changed, too. Please don't worry Dad. I know what I'm doing."

"Alright Morgan. You have my blessing."

Nick and I took our shot at a relationship three years ago. It worked perfectly in the beginning. He took me everywhere and introduced me to everyone. He made it his mission to help me recover from the chronic migraines I was experiencing. Under his care I recovered quickly and fully. It was the best gift I had ever received and I felt such gratitude for his eager willingness to help. I loved the man for the kindness I saw in his heart.

People and situations are complex, however. Around the eight-month mark, our relationship took on a new characteristic. Volatility. And that would've been a nice way of describing it. We had some altercations that bordered on major, not minor. Nick had a way of saying juuuust the right thing in juuuust the right way until I'd hit my personal snapping point.

Housework was usually the leading cause of strife.

Nick: "When you're (insert specific housework activity here) make sure to…"

A sentence that started this way never had a good ending for him. It was never *what* he was saying, it was *how* he was saying it. Condescending. He'd always have some sort of nitpicky way of doing anything. If you weren't doing it his way, he'd have something to say about it.

Morgan: "You are soooo nitpicky! I don't understand you."

Nick: "I'm not nitpicky. I've thought about the best way to do things for a lot of years. I am older than you. I want them done right."

Morgan: "Then do it yourself or get a mail order bride!!!"

But inevitably I would still do it because I really wanted the relationship to work and thought I wouldn't be able to find someone as compatible with me again. He was basically supporting me financially then, too, and I felt obligated because of that as well.

His argument was that I should want to help him out around the house, since we were "teammates." He said I was "entitled" and I will admit to that. My parents always took care of most things for me. I had my areas to work on. But doing things the way he wanted them done, entitled or not, was incredibly hard to swallow. So most of the time, I rebelled.

He questioned my competence around basic household tasks,

"You don't know how to use a vacuum cleaner and that's just not going to fly with me, Morgan!"

After I heard that one, I flew into one of the angriest moments of my life.

"What!!!!! Who do you think you are? I *KNOW* how to use a vacuum cleaner plus I'm sweeping *YOUR* floor! Have you taken into account that your vacuum cleaner may be the problem?"

I couldn't wrap my mind around how barbaric this mindset was. Then when I'd try to explain how I felt, he wouldn't listen. He'd just talk over me, louder then louder then…

"SHUT THE FUCK UP!"

Once those words came out of his mouth, I would resort to physically attacking and slightly injuring him in some way. I could NOT handle NOT being heard. He would threaten to call his friend who was a police officer to come bring me to jail. He'd scroll through his contact list and act like he was going to hit dial. One time he did, but we got things under control before he could answer.

Inevitably, after a serious altercation like this, I'd cry and beat myself up for days. He'd take me back, we'd drink, and then something else crazy would happen. Another pattern.

Two weeks before my 25th birthday, during a very intense fight, came the straw that broke the camel's back booming from his mouth,

"YOUR LIFE IS MINUSCULE IN COMPARISON TO MINE, MORGAN!"

And with that, I jumped out of his truck and never looked back, until now, three years later, when it all seemed new again.

CHAPTER 11
SOMEBODY ELSE'S DREAM

My full-time desk job with Nick is pacified by the potential for something greater. Right now something greater looks like stepping out of the role of a receptionist and into my own health counseling service run from his office. So naturally today, on my day off, there's a little spring in my step. I've been dreaming about my plan for this day and what I will do with myself and the $200 I have to my name.

The first stop is right outside of Nick's door. Even though Scenic Hill is a little bit run down, there's a flower in the middle of it all. It's called Tulip Cafe. I used to basically live at this cafe the first time I unsuccessfully cohabitated with Nick. The tiny little cafe is owned by two women who were brewing kombucha and making kimchi long before it became popular. It is homey, healthy, unique and delicious. Right up my alley.

I jog to their door, except, something is off. The building doesn't look the same. I google Tulip Cafe. Results: CLOSED.

I'm hungry but that's beside the point. This place was awesome and different and a breath of fresh air. Why didn't Tulip survive here? Why didn't Pittsburgh support its growth?

Walking back to my Jeep I return a missed phone call from Claire. She's recently met a man who she talks about as being "THE ONE." He's light-hearted, humorous, kind, has a good job, and is really, *really* into her.

"I've never heard you talk about a man like this, Claire. How do you know that he *is* the one?"

"Well you know how they say that you just know? Well, you just know."

I pretend as if her comment hadn't stuck me deep in a place I couldn't even describe to myself and tell her, "I am so happy for you! It's finally happening huh?!"

Driving south on the bridges to Lawrenceville, I ponder the "you just know" piece that Claire offered to me. Her concept sounds so idealistic, fairytale-ish even, such an easy theory to shrug off. But as much as I'd *love* to shrug it off, for some reason I can't. Claire and I have been talking men for 10 years solid and the certainty I just heard in her voice, the knowingness that she holds for this man, is so very different than I've ever heard her express before. I cannot deny that this is a new experience for her. I also cannot deny how her words reached me at the core because I don't "just know" and wondered if I ever would.

Lawrenceville calls me home again, distracting me from the larger issue at hand, to an appointment at another place that's ahead of its time in Pittsburgh: an organic hair salon. The owner inspires me because she had the strength to open something different than anything else in this area and it's working. Plus, she always has a smile on her face. The salon is perfect. Exposed brick, shabby chic white decor, wood accents, and a picture of a huge white horse above a fireplace. I love coming here.

I'm going about my regular routine. My color is processing. I'm reading a magazine article about Lady Gaga. I'm not expecting anything and I'm certainly not expecting an out-of-body experience today. But that's exactly what happens. It starts as I watch Lady Gaga's quote bounce off of the page and land straight in my body where I feel the chills start to develop,

"You *have* to understand, I was a waitress five years ago."

I can barely keep myself from bouncing off the chair. I'm blown away! How could such a massive change occur in such a short period of time? This world is full of undreamed-of possibilities! Every part of my body is awake and alive with the truth.

I snap back into reality right around the time my hair is finished. The fulfilled and happy owner of the salon is speaking to me. She's asking me about my life.

"What's new?"

"Well, my boyfriend and I just opened a holistic health center in Barraine."

I'm aware that it's *me* talking about *my* life but I feel oddly disconnected from the whole thing.

"You got exactly what you wanted then!" she says.

I nod but I'm out of my body again. I asked for a serious relationship, a career that I can enjoy, and just overall stability. I got all of those things. Now why in the world does it feel like I'm living somebody else's dream life?

CHAPTER 12
THE FIRST TASTE OF CREATIVE FREEDOM

I'm trying to choke down a disgustingly sweet martini at an overpriced, dimly lit, Barraine restaurant. On a whim, I had given the bartender the liberty to create a drink for me which ended up having more sugar, food dye, and preservatives than alcohol. So I set it down and look over at Nick,

"What should we do now?"

Since it's Friday night, what I'm really asking is: should we go out to the bar or not? We both check our phones a couple more times to see if our drinking friends are doing anything we haven't already done a million times before. Most of them are in the South Side at a bar you actually could not pay me to walk into again. Even though it's kind of a scene with tight dresses and blazers and valet, it's really quite boring. Based on the options, we decide it's not worth it.

So the night takes a different course. All of a sudden and without much rational thought, we are in Best Buy again. There's never a reason quite convincing enough for me to be in Best Buy. Ever. But I'm here nonetheless. Nick likes to look at electronics until I get to the point of tweaking out from the invasive flashing of a thousand televisions and the EMFs shooting in every direction.

I don't know what has happened to me lately. I am so go with the flow, I barely recognize my own patience. Maybe this is what being in a healthy relationship is all about? Haven't I heard people talking about "compromise" as being a healthy component of a relationship? I know he's enjoying himself but I'm fantasizing about the cozy red fleece blanket and my stack of books in his living room.

"Nick, I think I'll go sit in the car."

"I'm right behind you, Morgan," although I knew the lure of the noise and lights would keep him there a while.

In the car I ponder an idea that I've kind of always had since childhood. In my 6th grade English class, I wrote a book about death. My grandma had recently died and I knew my English teacher had recently lost her husband. So I wrote a tragic yet hopeful story that was met with much acclaim by both my teacher and the school librarian. I barely expected an "A" let alone their adamant recommendation to my mother that we look into publishing. We didn't publish but I never did forget their encouragement which planted a seed inside of me all those years ago, a seed that was beginning to sprout.

The drive home is fairly quiet until I decide to finally come out with it,

"So Nick, I don't know if I've ever told you this but someday I'd like to write a book."

"Really? Me too! Maybe we could co-author a book together!"

"Maybe, but I'm not totally sure about that. It's something that I may need to do on my own. There's something in me that is longing so deeply to be expressed."

"You have just as much potential as anyone Morgan. The key is actualizing it."

"Then there's something I need to ask you Nick. There's something that's been circling around in my mind. I need to know, that when this day comes, whatever I need to write will not be filtered by you. I need the guarantee of this creative freedom. Please tell me that you will be okay with this and not try to get in the way."

Irritated and possibly a little hurt he responds, "Yes, Morgan. Of course you can write what you want."

And from here, the remaining 20-minute car ride back to the city is filled with icy, cold silence.

CHAPTER 13
THIS ISN'T THE LIFE

The creative ways people figure out how to add alcohol into the mix never ceases to amaze me. Today there's a party that starts at 8:00 a.m., yes 8 a.m., at a friend of friend's house in Barraine. It starts at this hour for no good reason other than these people love drinking.

Nick and I arrive a little later, 3:00 p.m., due to a minor disagreement over my shirt. I totally like my shirt. The holdup is, he doesn't. I just got this shirt from the consignment store and it feels like one of the only shirts I own that makes me feel like myself. It's red, it's boho, and it's different.

Once we arrive, we attempt to catch up to the people who have been drinking for the last seven hours which is impossible because we are in a sea of 9-5, 30-somethings who are completely unfulfilled with their lives. By 5:00 the party is over. The once-so-enthusiastic voices yelling, "Fireball shots!" are passed out on couches. I am also loose lipped, apparently, because something slips out of my mouth that I didn't know I was feeling.

The home we're in belongs to a successful young couple who are about our age. Their lifestyle is my exact definition of what you are "supposed to do" when you grow up: buy a house in the suburbs that looks exactly like everyone else's while working a job that you barely like just to keep putting more stuff in the house that you don't really need but keep buying because everyone else has it. It feels like running on a hamster wheel with a blindfold on.

I can't hold it in any longer,

"Nick, this life isn't for us."

Luckily he's far enough away not to hear. Somehow, in my drunken state, I come to the epiphany that this life is the life we are actively trying to build. So I pour another drink.

———————————————

Later, dehydrated and dizzy, trying my best not to disturb Nick, I stumble out of bed to the living room. Another evening where I wish I wouldn't have drunk, now I'm awake at 3:00 a.m. feeling like half of a version of myself. But I have a dream to record in my journal that I've got to get down…

Back in my high school volleyball game. Outside hitter. Close game. The fire within me fully ignited. I knew without a shadow of a doubt that if the setter set me, I would kill it. So I told the setter to set me the ball. Our coach told the setter to set me the ball. Then for some reason, all of a sudden, the second string was in the game. I was watching the game from the sidelines. I wanted so badly to direct my internal blaze, but I couldn't! But I remember now. I remember that hunger.

It's been in me all along! It's who I am. And I don't want to wait any longer. I have gifts to share and people to share them with. SET ME THAT FREAKING BALL!

Another happy patient walks to the counter with Nick. This woman, in particular, claiming that Nick was the only one who could help her get her health back on track. They really do love him. And it's hard not to. He's obsessed with what he does, a perpetual smile beams from his face, and he genuinely cares about the people who walk through the door. When I see the impact he has on all of these people's lives I find a new level of attraction towards him. Then, when he brings them to the counter and says,

"This is Morgan. She'll get you all taken care of. Morgan is actually my girlfriend." My heart warms for this man who has so openly brought me into his life.

Nick lives and breathes this work. He'd stay at the office all night if I didn't remind him it was time to go home and go to sleep. His life purpose is so clear and defined that it's hard not to be a little jealous. I watch him take patients in and out of his office as I sit behind a desk trying to understand how to bill insurance companies.

But I'm on board with his vision to grow and expand his business. He's made me feel like an important part of it each and every step of the way. I know how lucky I am to have somebody trust me enough to bring me into their dream. I also know that it is his greatest desire for us to see eye to eye and work on this mission together. The ideal of a brilliant future and a family keep me enthusiastic enough to show up 40 hours a week.

Because it's Christmas Eve, I have a little easier time peeling Nick away from work today. Christmas Eve, after all, is the biggest day of the year for my Italian family. But I do not get excited about Christmas anymore. After Santa no longer existed I looked for that magic fairy dust feeling again in the euphoria of being in love. I thought maybe Christmas could be magical again if I had a man to share it with. But Christmas after Christmas passed with maybe a mere text message from Dex saying, "Merry Christmas, Bear!" and I got to the point where I needed to decondition myself from the high and hopeful expectations that I held around Christmas with a new man. So this night, needless to say, is a monumental night for myself and the many Italian women who have been awaiting Nick's arrival.

My huge family is gathered around a long table filled with a variety of pasta and fish. There are three gluten-free options out of the 50, one of which is vino. The volume level is as high as a Vegas nightclub. Nick is next to me engaged and laughing with my uncle. I turn to my 90-year-old, 5-foot-tall, Aunt Carlotta.

"Well, here he is," I speak to her with a little smile on my face.

She knows EXACTLY what I'm talking about. She's been praying to St. Jude*for years that I would find my husband.

Her eyes light up with satisfaction.

The crowd disperses to get ready for midnight mass and Nick and I head to my bedroom to exchange gifts. I found myself really unsure of what to get Nick this year so I chose gifts that seemed to be the most practical.

He unwraps his first gift which is a crock pot. A couple months ago I heard him saying that he may like having one. So I bought the best one I could find. His reaction, however, is less than optimal,

"Oh, that's nice."

Strike one. I'm hoping that this next gift will be my ace in the hole then. It takes him hours to iron all of his work shirts so I figured, why not get him a fancy steam iron to save him some time? As he tears into it and realizes it's a steam iron, I watch as his eyes glaze over.

"Thank you."

"You're welcome. You may not realize it now but this gift will come in handy!" I assure him.

---

* *St. Jude is considered the saint of impossible causes in the Catholic tradition.*

Then, it's my turn. He hands me two huge boxes. I rip into them both to find something quite odd. Luggage. A small purple suitcase and a large purple suitcase.

"Does the size work?"

"Well, yes."

"This is great quality luggage. Look, it's really easy to maneuver." He pulls them around on the hardwood in my bedroom.

"Do you like them?"

"Yes." I pause for a second to try to fathom what just happened. We gave each other gifts that were *usable*. Then I remember to be polite. "Yes of course I like them. Thank you, Nick. They're perfect."

Chapter 15
Whose Schedule Is It?

February 3, 2014

Last night, I dreamt that I was walking though the grocery store and came to the realization that the next person who annoyed me, I was going to sock right in the face. This is also when I realized that I may have some pent-up anger to deal with.

"Nick, I think I need to cut back on my hours at the office. Laura needs them more than I do and she's better at the job than I am anyway. Plus, the business has grown to the point where you don't need me here full time anymore. I need a little more freedom to do the things that make me happy outside of work."

"All right Morgan, let's give it a try."

We decide on a schedule of 12 hours per week and my life turns into pure magic! My days consist of reading, studying for nutrition school, introspection, meditating, and cooking. I get excited for the time I have alone. I relish in it. I start creating a website. I begin to get a better idea of Morgan. I am happy and content.

But after two weeks of freedom, Nick walks through the door to a warm dinner on the table and expresses his resentment,

"Morgan, there are more things that you need to be learning at the office. You should be there."

Then before I get the chance to sock him in the face he says, "I don't expect you to stay as a receptionist once you finish school. At that point you can start taking clients at the office." But to still maintain some control he made sure to point out, "Don't forget, it's time for you to start learning how to be a professional."

I thought I was a professional? Maybe I don't want to be a "professional" by his definition. Maybe I don't want to listen to him at all.

After two hours of fighting tooth and nail in bed, the decision was made, that the next day, I would go back to the office, back on his schedule.

The energy has to be right at the office so the patients feel good when they're here. So the fact that the last thing in the world I want to do is take direction from Nick is a problem.

"I have the best intentions for both of us. This business is my dream and I want you to feel a part of it."

When he says this, I ease into the idea. My heart melts a little. I remember why I love him. I remember it feels comfortable and good to be here. So I relinquish and we start anew.

The pattern begins again. We coexist in harmony for a week or so. Our conscious minds forget the unresolved chaos. I'm cooking, I'm smiling, we're laughing. Then Dex calls me. Then texts me. Then emails me. And every single time I feel a responsibility to tell Nick. Every single time his face turns red with anger. Every single time the unresolved chaos resurfaces. And every single time I feel some sort of obligation to answer Dex.

Why is he so persistent? I push off the response as long as I can. Until finally, I return the call:

DEX: "Where have you been?"

MORGAN: "I left my job at the nonprofit. I'm working with Nick now. I helped him open his new office in Barraine. My schedule is really full right now so I won't be able to film anytime soon if that's why you're calling."

DEX: "I'm biting my tongue so hard that it just fell off."

And we don't get much further than that. I laugh because it's kind of funny but I also feel my stomach turn.

I'm beginning to have strange and vivid dreams. One of a place I've never been, filled with flowers and sunshine and happy people walking in the morning. I ask out loud, "can I stay here?" And hear the response, "yes." When I awake I jot it down in my journal:

The location seemed like California. I can't believe people live somewhere with such great weather.

I've picked up a new morning routine also. It's called morning pages. I learned this exercise through a lecture by Julia Cameron* at my school. First thing in the

---

* *Julia Cameron an American author, artist, poet, playwright, novelist, filmmaker, composer, and journalist. She is most famous for her book* The Artist's Way *in which she advises readers to write morning pages.*

morning, without judgement or overthinking it, I longhand write three pages in a notebook. The purpose is to access some deeper part of myself to bring out true messages and to get into creative flow. Tapping in in this way is what I live for. The mystical, the unseen, the magic has always been my greatest passion.

While listening to Julia speak, I receive a pretty blatant intuitive nudge. My body becomes completely alive again, just like the experience with the Lady Gaga quote. It feels as if I've awakened into a beautiful world after a long sleep. Her two little words made me pause the entire lecture and stare:

"Sight unseen"

As Julia spoke about following her creative dreams and moving somewhere new in pursuit of her passions, my hearing intensified. She explained how she moved "sight unseen" to a place she had never been because she felt called to go. I underlined the words. I circled the words. They jumped off my notebook like a soft flash of light. And they embedded themselves right into my consciousness for some unknown reason.

Something is happening to me and I'm not sure what. These experiences are so surreal and I'm not sure why.

"I need you to film again."

I return Dex's call after weeks of no contact.

"I'm really not sure how I'm going to pull that off, Dex. Every time we do, Nick and I almost break up. This has to be the last time."

"Okay, we will get all the material we need and this can be the last time. "

Now, to break this to Nick. I wait until the day is done at the office. I've learned my lesson on this one. Anytime I've tried talking to Nick about anything regarding Dex, the day gets jacked up every time. I already feel like I'm causing enough havoc in his professional life. I don't need to rock the boat anymore.

I walk into the living room like a child who just broke a window. He can sense what's coming. I don't even need to say it.

"Nick. He said this will be the last time. I'll do this now and get it out of the way. This will be it. "

"This *has* to be it Morgan. I'm ready to wash my hands of this. I'm ready to move on with our lives."

Just like that, the last filming date is set. And just like that, Nick and I have an invisible tension between us.

I hit Nick with this news on a Friday. On Saturday the invisible tension turns to visible tension in words and scowls and fights coming from seemingly nowhere, except we really know where it's coming from. By Sunday, I am so distressed that I'm not sure if I can handle it. I'm hearing cryptic messages from my body begging me to change my course of action before the stress levels become unbearable. So Sunday morning I tell Nick I'm going to church. Alone.

The snow falls so slowly around me. It crunches under my tires as I put my Jeep into drive. The softness of the white falls all around my car, filling the day with a silent stillness that no sound can break. West on I-376 for 10 minutes and I pull into the tiny parking lot of a place I haven't been for a while. I walk into the musty, dilapidated house, into a small blue living room. Twenty chairs face east towards a small altar filled with pictures of ancient men. Five people sit throughout the room, spines straight, eyes closed. I sit down in the front of the room, as close to the huge picture of Paramahansa Yogananda as possible. He's wearing an orange robe, a smile gleaming in his eyes. I don't even have to settle in because just like that, all of the tension leaves my body. I stare at this picture. I close my eyes. All of the pain, all of the suffering from the past couple weeks is gone. Everything is okay right here in this moment. I become very still. I become very peaceful. I sit here like this for an hour.

I walk out of the house slowly as the people smile around me. I realize that the most important thing in my life has been the one thing that has been missing. I make a sacred quiet promise to myself. This is why I am here. This life has a very different path than the one that I've been taking.

CHAPTER 18
A MUCH BIGGER DREAM

I've begun meditating every morning and every night. I diligently do morning pages every day, which feels a lot like getting my act together on paper. Each spare moment I have, my eyes are glued to books written by the wisest people who've ever lived. I spend time in nature, alone.

My dreams are becoming more vivid. I record them in the morning. Last night I dreamt about a road. In this dream I was in front of a group of children whom I was teaching. I was told to draw a picture that best represented me. I drew a road.

As soon as I wake up I tell Nick about the dream.

"I think the road means that I like to travel," I tell him.

"You're weird." Then he laughs and springs out of bed to get ready.

I head straight to my notebook:

March 5, 2014

I told Nick my dream about the road and he joked that I was weird - I told him the road means I like to travel. But it's more than that. The road is a freedom, an outward and inward journey. The ability to up and leave and explore. And it's something I don't quite feel I have right now. With money, I would.

I put on my shoes and head straight out the door. My senses have intensified. I'm aware of the pavement beneath me. I wind through the familiar streets, past the children on bicycles along the graffitied alleys. Their curse words don't fit their innocent little bodies.

The street becomes more narrow. I smell stale cigarettes coming from musty old houses. The houses that dot this side of Scenic Hill have the most expansive views of the rivers, the boat docks, the Pittsburgh neighborhoods, and the skyscrapers. They sit above all of it. They are houses that could've been something, that used to be something, and are now long forgotten and abused.

There are boards on the windows and boards on the doors and foreclosure signs hanging everywhere. Except for one, where a 30-year-old man stumbles out the front door in a fog of smoke. He doesn't care to notice me. Squinting at the sunlight, he lights a cigarette and walks towards the city with no intention of adjusting the jeans that are falling below his waist.

The bar on the side of the hill, with one of the best city views in the world, has one of the most depressed interiors. Inside, noon appears to be midnight. The only thing lighting the small room is a glowing orange Coors Light sign. As the door opens, natural light pours in on the five locals crouched over their ashtrays. They are the only people brave enough to be here. I wish that they would walk outside to the freedom of the beautiful views below.

But I don't judge the scene. I never have. I embrace how different even this part of the city is from the small town in which I grew up. I look around and feel it. There is beauty even in the complete dilapidation of an entire neighborhood. And I keep walking until I get to my spot.

I arrive at the Scenic Hill lookout point that I discovered when I lived at Nick's the first time, at age 24. I step through broken bottles to a small opening where the trees and the overgrowth part away to the view below. Downtown Pittsburgh is stretched before me with all its skyscrapers, buildings and hills. The North Side neighborhood with its tall houses and chimneys is on my right. Cars move in and out of the city along the curved highway.

My spot. My point of transition three years ago. It is much more overgrown now but the view is still clear. This view used to excite me. I had never lived in a city. I imagined what this city could possibly hold for me. I would hear a voice say, "No one can tell you not to look down at this city and dream." So I went off into that city and did what I could. I dreamt myself away from Nick and into the arms of men who never held too tightly. I learned and played and explored and got hurt.

A lot. But I never saw myself coming back here, pondering the same vantage point. And now, for some reason, here I am. Three years later, here I am, looking out over the same point, instead of with excitement, this time with fear.

Where has the dreamer gone? Who is she now? Has she really allowed herself to be so tainted by the experiences that hurt her that she doesn't know what her dreams are anymore?

No, the dreamer is still here and she is dreaming somewhere deep inside of her. And she knows that something is stirring in her heart. And she knows that something is about to shift. She does not want to live between two worlds in either a life she'd be happy to settle on or a world in which bigger and more profound things may be able to happen in ways she's not even quite sure yet.

She walks back to the life she created. She walks back to her mind. She walks back to the fear. She walks back to the people who are afraid as well. But she walks back with something new inside of her. Just as the overgrown lookout point makes way for the view of the city, so too has she witnessed her heart amongst the overgrowth of fear. And this time, she has a much bigger dream.

Chapter 19
The Journey Ahead

Countryhaven is my next stop. I'm charged up, fired up, I need someone to listen.

"I need to get in my car and just go, Mom! I need to travel. I kind of just want to start driving."

I'm lying on my back in my parents' living room, wooden cathedral ceilings high above. This is the dream house I asked for when I was 13.

My mom, hearing the words and noticing the electricity in my voice, is taken off guard, pauses, then replies,

"Maybe we could go visit Dreama and Hank in Palm Springs."

This idea pacifies me until midday when I'm curled in Nick's bed praying for some clarity.

There's no way to prepare him for the crazy ideas that keep popping through my mind. And there's no easy way to begin this conversation. But I ask him to join me anyway holding his hand to soften the blow.

"I have this feeling, Nick, like I need to get in my car and go somewhere. Down the east coast, or somewhere."

Taken off guard, I feel him back away. He removes his hand from mine. His smiling eyes turn serious.

"What are you talking about, Morgan?"

"I can't explain it. I don't know what's happening to me, Nick. But there's something that feels untapped inside of me."

If I could only put into words these feelings coming from a place I've never accessed before. If I could only understand myself right now.

"Have you thought about the logistics of this trip? How you will afford it? How many days of work you'll miss? Where you're even going?"

"Well, not really. I haven't figured out any of the details yet. I just have this feeling, ya know, like there's a journey I need to take."

I was hoping for compassion but not exactly expecting it. "Your idea doesn't make any sense, Morgan."

Even though his words seem harsh, I can feel the deeper truth. My longing for something more does not involve him at all. I can see the hurt man behind the anger. Warm tears begin running down my face.

"I don't want you to be sad, Morgan. If this is something you need to do, then it's something you need to do. But we can make things work here. We can be happy here. Don't you like the life we have together?"

"Yes, I do like it here, Nick. It's everything I've ever wanted. You gave me everything. But the thought of this journey isn't going away."

"Are you coming back?"

He's holding me now, his eyes somehow filled with compassion, my body motionless and frozen, my voice completely silent. I cannot utter the word he wants to hear, even though I see how much this man loves me. It would be so easy just to say yes right now. Even though I love him, I've got no answer for him.

This man, this life, is everything I've been actively trying to find for the last three years. Now I've got it right here in front of me. All I have to do is say yes. All I have to do is grab his strong arms and pull him towards me. But I cannot for the life of me utter a sound. All I can do is cry.

Chapter 20
The Choice

We coexist in harmony for the next few days, not speaking about the silly idea I had to go exploring without a rational plan. We talk about the possibility of a vacation to somewhere warm together, maybe a trip to the Virgin Islands. We only have one more thing to get out of the way now: my last day of filming with Dex.

When I leave the office and kiss Nick goodbye, I try to hide my excitement. Nick seems to be taking this last day of filming okay. So the last thing I need him to see is that I'm actually charged up to go do it. I'm assuming he's visualizing a light at the end of a tunnel and to never ever hear Dex's name again.

At 5:30 p.m. I practically sprint to my car. Then I call Dex who is back in Pittsburgh now to film these scenes with me.

"I'm on my way Dex! I had a little trouble getting out of the office."

"Morgan, you *have* to get out of that relationship."

Whoa. Stomach jolt.

"Dex let's stick to business."

"No. I'm serious, Morgan. If you never listen to me again, that's okay. This advice is more important than any advice I've ever given to you. Please trust me."

"Thanks for your opinion. He loves me. I love him. I'm happy. I'm not going to talk about this with you. Now let's be professional."

I drive towards the city on Route 79. I know this man well enough to know that, when he has a point, he's going to make it. I'm on the other end of the line, and for some reason, I'm listening. But it's painful.

"You can do anything you want in the world. The only reason you're making this choice is out of fear and desperation. "

"Now hold on a second. I'm not desperate, Dex! You're taking this too far."

The directness in his voice demands that I listen.

"Without a doubt, sweetheart, you are completely desperate, and I'm here to tell you that you have no reason to be. You don't think you have any other options. You can't see this right now but you've got a million options! You have a limited perspective and you are listening to the people around you who also have a limited perspective. In fact, *you're* the one who told me that if you had a million dollars that you wouldn't be in the relationship you're in."

"I mean, I don't think I meant it like that. I believe I said I'd travel."

"Same thing."

I pull into my parking spot outside of Nick's house. I'm stopping here first in order to get changed for filming. My eyes are transfixed on a 100-year-old brick townhouse and my body is not moving. I don't like what he's saying but I'm not telling him to stop.

"I was talking to my friend Travis about you. I told him about the situation you are in and how I couldn't figure out why you would even allow it. He had some good advice. He said, "Women for the most part don't know how to go out into the world and get what they want. That's why they settle. Men on the other hand, in general, know how to go get the things that they want.""

"This is not really making sense because this *is* what I want. My life *is* good. I'm with a man who loves me who I'm compatible with. I've been given the opportunity to work in a career field that I love."

"You're lying to yourself, sweetheart. You're not too old. It's not too late. There's no such thing. You've got blinders on and you don't realize your own potential. I don't think this is what you want to be doing for work, either. I don't really see you working at a doctor's office."

I'm finally able to move my legs after the shock of what Dex is saying to walk inside Nick's house. His living room is dimly lit and for some reason, unwelcoming.

Dex is still on my ear.

"I don't feel like I handled things with us the best I could. I think I fucked up your mindset on the way you believe a relationship should be, Morgan. I didn't want to be controlling with you, but control was the only thing you responded to."

My heart drops. I can't believe what I'm hearing. I can't believe that he's weeping. Is it true? Did I want to be controlled? I sit down on the couch. When he goes to talk again, he barely can.

"Please Morgan, please trust me right now. You have no idea how bad of a situation you're in. You need to get out of that relationship. You don't understand fully right now, but someday you will. As you grow, what you want will grow. Just trust that this is true. You are about to fuck up your life."

I'm spinning right along with his words. I feel myself unlatch, the same way that the tears stream down his face. Then a voice I didn't know belonged to me, made an agreement I didn't know I could,

"Okay Dex, I'll leave. It's okay. I'll leave," I whisper.

"Oh, thank God," he exhales.

Then I continue,

"I don't know how to do this. Can I move away? I want to move away. I'm not sure how, I only have $63 in my bank account. I could ask my cousin to lend me…"

"I'll give you the money."

"What?"

"I'll give it to you. I feel partly responsible for the situation you're in."

"I'll pay you back."

"No. I don't want it. This is my attempt to make things right. But I never want to talk again after I give it to you. I can't handle the responsibility of your life anymore. It's too much. I don't want it. You need to be able to do things on your own from this point on."

He's still crying, and although I'm hurt from his last statement, some part of me knows that I have to respect it.

I'm back in my car very quickly because this conversation doesn't seem like an appropriate one to be having in Nick's living room.

Five minutes later, I pull up outside of the Renaissance, the decided upon location for filming. The plan is that Dex will be in his condo 10 minutes away directing me from FaceTime as the cameraman films the scene of me in the hotel. We will not be in the same physical location this evening.

Our conversation continues. There is so much energy and so much momentum behind every word.

"I could drive my Jeep down the east coast, although I'm not sure it will make it that far. It's pretty old. Then maybe find a place I'd like to live? Charleston is nice, maybe I'll live there."

"Is Charleston your first choice?"

I have to really ponder this question. I pause.

"Well, I mean, my first choice would probably be California but that's really far away and it's really expensive to live…"

"Don't take distance or cost of living into account. You are choosing the place where you want to live. Take your first choice. How silly is it not to choose what you really want when it comes to something so important as where you live."

Good point. I always assumed I'd have to compromise, somewhere close enough, somewhere cheap enough. I was lying to myself again.

"Okay my first choice would be a coastal town in California!"

"Yes, that sounds more like you!"

I walk into the hotel where I'm supposed to be meeting Dex's cameraman Justin. I look around but don't see him anywhere.

"Where's Justin?"

"I told him we are running late," Dex says. "This conversation is more important than anything."

So I sit down on the sofa in the lobby of the Renaissance Hotel. Dex sits in his condo. Two more hours go by. Time seems to halt. I hear myself making plans to break up with Nick and move away as if I'm actually going to. With each breath and each word, the floor of the hotel lobby becomes more vivid. My senses completely heightened. Big red, yellow and blue squares go in and out of focus. People are walking in and out of the elevator. The doors open with a chime. My heart beating. I hear myself talk about moving my things out of Nick's. Dex is listening to my plan, offering guidance and motivation.

I look at the clock and realize that Dex and I have been on the phone for almost eight hours straight. Because of the magnitude of what's happening, eight hours has felt like one minute.

"How am I going to do this D? I have to go back to Nick's house *tonight*. He thinks we are filming right now. It's close to 1 a.m. I'm scared to think that he might know what's actually going on."

"Text him right now and tell him filming ran late."

"Then what?"

"Then just get out of there as quickly as you can. "

—————————————

A chill runs down my spine as I stand outside Nick's house, reaching quietly for the door knob. I walk in slowly. He pretends to be asleep. I pretend that the whole earth hadn't just shifted. Not a word is exchanged. Not a word is needed. The feeling of pure, red, anger emanating from that bedroom said it all. I lie there quietly next to him, fearful that he may know that there hadn't been one moment of filming that took place this evening. Wide awake and unmoving I lie there, doing my best to hide that tomorrow, I am going to leave.

CHAPTER 21
I AM FREE.

This morning I have become an actress. My alarm goes off and I pretend as if I had been sleeping. I get ready and pretend as if it is just another normal day. I make the bed the same way. I brush my teeth the same way. But I speak very, very little to Nick other than, "Would you like some fish oil?" and "I'll meet you at the office." He makes it easy with his own silence born from his dissatisfaction with my surprisingly late night. We know we have things to say to each other but we're not saying them now.

I follow behind him in my car. The 20-minute drive north to Barraine is much welcomed. I need to process.

I pull into the Starbucks off the Barraine exit. I did not sleep in fact, so I'm supplementing with caffeine. Although I kind of know that I do not need it. There's enough adrenaline running through my body to do anything right now.

I step into civilization, into a room full of people going about their routine. I realize that very soon I will not have a routine like the rest of them. I stand in line but the world feels like a different place—like a place I no longer fit into the same way. How could I fit into a place that I am about to reject everything I have that everybody wants?

I look down at my body to make sure I'm clothed, to make sure I'm not in a dream that I'm walking through public naked. I am keenly aware that I am disconnected from my body and peering from the outside in. The other customers must be able to notice that something strange is going on. That the girl beside them has to remind herself to walk, talk and pay for her drink. But it really doesn't matter how I'm looking or acting. I'm too charged to be insecure right now.

I arrive at the office and set up for the day. Three sips of the coffee and my heart is already beating too fast. The caffeine is too much this morning. But the patient files are in place, voicemails checked, and the waiting room is tidied. Nick doesn't say a word.

No one really saw it coming. Not even me. He takes the first patient back with him. I am alone. But as my fingers begin to type, "Dream Beach Towns in California," I let them move. Click. Scrolling, scrolling, scrolling. My eyes dart from word to word, coming to life with each new click of the mouse. Here comes Nick and the patient towards the desk. No! Minimize.

"That will be $30 today. See you next time." Does my voice sound any different? Am I giving anything away?

He takes his next patient back.

Maximize. I'm clicking through a slider:

Avalon...San Clemente...Dana Point. No.

Carpinteria...Solana Beach...Venice. No.

Laguna...Newport...Encinitas.

Encinitas. Encinitas? Sounds familiar.

A patient in the waiting room walks towards me. Minimize. I have no idea what she just asked me but I smile and say yes. She sits back down. Please, people, no more questions.

Why does Encinitas sound so familiar? I keep reading faster than I've ever read in my life. The pictures are stunning of the oceans, and surfers, and cliffs.

I read an interview. "At the risk of sounding a little out there, this town has a great energy."

Words jump off the page: "Healing, yoga, health food, art, ocean, mind-body-spirit." This is good.

It appears the town has a major attraction: a vast meditation garden. I click. Wait. I know this place! Of course I know this place! This is the town Yogananda spoke about in the book that completely changed my life, *Autobiography of a Yogi!* This is the town he had lived in! The meditation gardens were his creation years ago! My God, this is it. Encinitas is my town!

An ecstatic electricity runs through my body. I delete the web page history. My morning shift is over. He's still in the back room with a patient. Perfect. Ever

this letter would take a significant amount of time but as soon as the blank page appears before me, it is filled with words.

Next. My car is parked in front of the house, trunk open. I hesitate to leave my trunk open in this neighborhood and then realize it doesn't matter. I'm making trips between his unused second floor where my things are stored and the street. The floorboards of every stair creak as I pass. I have in my arms plates, bins, a dish rack, a speaker, a framed picture of The Beatles. I'm carrying all of it at once. Heavy things, light things: they all feel the same. There is no rain, no snow, no sleet, only sun and blue skies to lighten the load.

The neighbor asks me if I'm moving. This is only the second time he's ever spoken to me. I sit on the front stoop for a moment pondering if this is really happening. Before I can question too much, my feet begin to move back up the stairs to fetch another load of items. I just gave him a friendly nod.

I have one possession left in his house: my purple comforter and organic cotton sheets. Standing in the bedroom, I stare at it. No. It's too cruel to strip the bed. I will not take these. If I can leave with as little an upset or change in his world as possible - I will. The sheets are his.

It would be dark when he got home. I've been sitting absolutely still in the living room for 30 minutes.

Every 30 seconds I reconsider everything I've come to. I expect him by 7:15. At 7:47 I hear his shoes pound through the corridor. My heart is beating faster than his steps on the torn-up cement. I hear the lock in the door, then the turning of the knob, then the release as it swings open. I still have a few more seconds before he reaches the living room. I can still change my mind.

A gust of air moves past my face with a whiff of his earthy cologne as he walks in and we occupy the same space. I am sitting so tall, it must be deceiving, because I am shaking on the inside.

"What is it?"

But he already feels it.

My arms are weak, the blood draining from them. Just when I don't know if I'm going to hand him the letter I hear myself speak,

Dear Nick,

This letter comes from a place inside of me that I have just begun to discover. Our life together has been very beautiful. Thank you for welcoming me into your dream.

I realized that I have a dream too, and that dream is in California. This comes as a surprise to me as well. I cannot ignore this message. I may forever wish that I had made the leap when I had heard the call. I apologize so deeply for getting you tangled up in my own selfishness of not fully knowing what I wanted.

I've come to realize that my spiritual life is the most important thing to me. It's time for me to honor that. I'd like to be around people on a similar journey so I can learn and grow and listen to my soul.

You are right, I think it's time for me to grow up. So I'm ready to go carve my path in the world. Please know that I will forever be thankful for your love and your patience as I traveled through this process of self-discovery. I am so sorry for any hurt this may be causing, however I do love you and wish you well always.

Love,

Morgan

I can feel his resistance to my words. At the same time, I feel an exhalation of freedom coming from my mouth. I want to cry but I don't.

"This is definitely a sign," he says, referring to the text he received from an ex-girlfriend right in the middle of my letter.

There is pain and anger everywhere but I am completely here in this space—my attentiveness so required in a moment so volatile.

"Where are you moving?"

I hesitate to tell him. "Encinitas."

He takes the high ground, standing, escalating, then raising his voice. "I can't believe I got involved with you again. I should've known you'd do something like this."

He turns his attention towards his phone, anywhere but towards me, texting his friends and receiving rapid responses.

"She's crazy."

&

"You're better off."

They might be right but I don't know what to say. I can't apologize for what I've just read because it's how I feel. I can't say, "maybe we can come to a solution" because this is actually what I want. Instead I sit here and watch this good man struggle in front of me. His struggle comes out as anger right now but I know that it's pain. Pain for allowing me back in again. Pain for not fully understanding. And pain for thinking your life is going to be a certain way and then watching that idea walk out the door.

At 9:00 p.m., I walk out to my car into weather that is no longer welcoming. The rain has begun, the temperature has dropped and the ease of the sunny warm day has become hostile. I drive away from Scenic Hill as if I actually know what I'm doing, but the fact of the matter is, nothing seems clear anymore. I'm driving away from the life I thought I had always wanted. How is my foot still on the gas? The worst of it, though, is not this. The worst of it is bearing what I have just done to Nick. What will his life look like now? What will he tell the patients and his family? Will I ever be able to forgive myself for hurting him again?

I look into my rearview mirror at a trunk filled with things that have no meaning to me anymore. My possessions along with the rain impede my view. I don't really care. After what I have just done, the idea of dying feels more comfortable than the pain of living.

The 50-minute drive north to Countryhaven feels like a déjà vu nightmare. I don't care to arrive anyway. What will I do once I get there?

Driving back the long driveway, I turn off my headlights. I want no sign of my arrival. Into my childhood room I slip without so much as a peep. I turn off the lights. I tuck myself into bed. I curl into a ball. And I can't quiet my mind.

What have I done?

CHAPTER 23
AM I INSANE?

The next morning starts off with:

"He was going to marry you, Morgan! He was going to give you everything!!!!"

My mom is crying. She is shaking her head. She is in such disbelief.

Her reaction almost leads me to my iPhone, straight to Nick's name.

It's not long before my dad needs an explanation as to what's going on. The best thing I can think of in this moment is to read them the letter I wrote to Nick. This letter expresses what is true to me. So I ask them to sit down on the couch to listen. I begin reading the letter with such heartfelt compassion thinking that once they hear this, they will surely understand. As I reach the end, "Love, Morgan," I look up to both of them blinking at me.

"Morgan, not one word of that made sense," says my mom.

And I realize right here that this is going to be way harder than I thought.

I agree to a suggested therapy session. The therapist "really helped Jane with her anxiety."

"When can you go?" my mom asks.

"Well, really anytime." I literally have nowhere to be anymore, which is a pitiful realization.

My windshield wipers are on full blast as I pull in. It's still raining. Surprise. This is the second therapy session I've ever attended. The first was an anger management session that Dex strongly suggested I attend after launching his Xbox controller at his face.

As I shut off my car I remember a story about a man from Countryhaven who everyone thought went crazy, too. His children were pretty much grown, when one day, he disappeared. He told no one that he was leaving he just got in his car and left. They sent out a search party for him. The local newspaper ran an article. They considered him a missing man until he showed up in Countryhaven again.

The therapist lets me talk, which is good. I need to.

After about 15 minutes of unloading he begins. "It seems like you have your stuff together and have a good head on your shoulders. I just need to ask a couple more questions to rule out the possibility of bipolar."

What?? I'm panicking.

"Have you found yourself making erratic and illogical decisions in the past?"

Now wait a minute.

"I guess people have definitely questioned my decisions in the past."

"How so?"

"Well, I left a 'dream job' and jumped into another job that I thought I'd enjoy more. The new job didn't end up working whatsoever. Everyone was kind of shaking their heads then, too. Then I went into a five-month solitude in my parents' home which might have been classified as clinical depression. I'm not quite sure. I've never really looked up the definition. I just assumed I was probably depressed. I barely wanted to leave the house. I searched endlessly for my purpose on Earth. Oh my gosh, is there a possibility that I'm bipolar?"

"It doesn't seem like it. As a therapist, I just have to make sure."

The session is over. I give him whatever money my mom handed me and walk out. Great session. Now I've got a new worry: the very slight possibility that I may have a mental illness.

CHAPTER 24
NO ONE BUT ME

It may not be worth saving the money and living at home right now because it is a blurry, blurry hell being here. My mom bursts into tears at random moments. My dad tries to pacify my mom by asking that I come to my senses. I tell them I'm still going to move. There is not one moment of peace.

So I've got to go back to Pittsburgh to get the rest of my stuff from Nick's. Dex also asked me to film today, one last time, before I move. Anything to get me out of the house is welcomed. I don't care what it is.

Driving back through Scenic Hill is weird. The thought of walking back into his house is freaking me out. Luckily he's at the office so there is no chance of communication. As soon as I enter his home I can tell I need to do this quick. The house in some way is embedded with the energy of, "get out" so I'm hustling. All my stuff packed, I take one more breath here, then drop the little red key with the glued-on rhinestones in the slot. I shut the door—goodbye for good.

I am absolutely not using the luggage Nick got me for Christmas to move to California. Something is just not right about that. So I drive to the Fox Chapel TJ Maxx where I swap out the purple luggage for black. Since I have less money in the bank than it would take to buy a TJ Maxx suitcase, it turns out that Nick's Christmas gift was spot on after all.

By 8:00 p.m. I'm driving back to the hotel where the biggest decision of my life had been made a few days prior. I'm trying to hide my disappointment that Dex and I will not be occupying the same physical space this evening. He will be directing me remotely again from his Pittsburgh condo. The truth is I miss him. And I'd love his support right now during this vulnerable time in my life. But I'm not really getting what I want because I can see his face on a screen right in front of me but I can't touch it.

I'm doing as directed which never turns out the way he wants it until maybe the tenth time. Even then, it still kind of sucks.

"I'm not an actress!" I scream for the hundredth time. What I'm really screaming is, "Why aren't you here with me right now? I need you!" But I'm too vulnerable to actually communicate that in this moment.

"Just be yourself and stop trying to act," his deep voice demanding that I perform. "That's the only time it ever turns out good."

Easier said than done, especially when there's a camera in my face and the most intense, intelligent person I know playing director. Plus, half the time he wants me to look natural so any makeup I've put on, he asks that I wipe away. Every last insecurity I have comes up on his cameras.

Time is irrelevant when it comes to his projects. I learned that a long time ago. The first time we ever filmed, he predicted that it would take four hours to complete. But eight hours later, at 3:00 a.m. when the cameras actually turned off, my body begging for sleep, he was still talking to me about the film. Then 3:00 a.m. became 5:00 a.m. and I realized that this film was this man's life.

So tonight at 2:00 a.m. he is satisfied with the work. The cameraman starts to put his things away. Now it's just Dex and I on FaceTime together.

"I moved all my stuff out today. It's really happening," I tell him.

"You know, it's really late. I don't want you driving home tired. Go get a room for the night, put it on us."

"That's okay, I'll be fine driving."

"I think it's a better idea for you to stay."

I hesitate, hesitate, hesitate. But I know this could be the last time so I have to ask.

"Are you going to come over?"

"Babydoll," he says as if surprised by the innocence of my question. "I'll stop and say hi."

I'm fully awake again. I practically run to the hotel room and jump into the shower. I get myself ready and then hop into bed. I haven't seen Dex in months. The fact of the matter is, I'm excited to see him and I'm excited to be near him again. He is so close, his drive only 10 minutes. After 10 minutes pass, I close my eyes and try to sleep.

At 2:45 I'm the most eager fake sleeping person on the planet. Nothing will feel better right now than being held with all the stress at home and with the breakup...

At 3:15 his name lights up my phone.

"I'm in room 415!" I basically scream.

"I'm not here Morgan."

"What?"

"I'm not coming."

Nail in the coffin. My God, he's not coming. The tears pour from my body.

"Why?," I plead.

"I don't think it's a good idea. I want to more than anything, trust me. But you're just getting out of a relationship. We have a pattern of running to each other when we are in pain. I don't think it's healthy.

"Dex!"

"If you really need me to come, you know I will. I'll be there for you when you need me. But I do not want to get in the way of your personal growth."

Part of me has never fully understood him. Another part of me has. I knew what our love had felt like when we were in it. I knew it had moments of heaven on earth. But so many times it felt like the rug was being pulled out from under me. It felt like drowning most of the time.

His argument made sense to some degree. I could convince myself of this right now because in the back of my mind I had possible future hope for us. But the tears poured like a river. I could feel him struggling between what was right and what was easy in his mind. But in this moment, there was no difference to me.

"Please, Dex," I ask him for the last time. My body pauses awaiting his response. My heart jumps in anticipation. Then somewhere in between an inhale and an exhale I hear,

"I'm not ready."

Three words: the message he had been telling me all along that I refused to hear. Now, there is no choice but to acknowledge it. He's not ready and he's not coming. I'd always assumed that he was ready and that he would show up. But I had assumed too much. The hope for a utopian life, that idealistic vision for our relationship that he held, always kept me in place.

During the hardest week of my life I'm being dealt yet another challenge. I've never experienced so many huge transitions all at once. I've never felt so vulnerable in my entire life. It hurts maybe more than I ever really have. I'm withstanding more than I ever knew I was capable of. And you know what, lying in this bed, I'm still alive and I'm still breathing. Someway, somehow, I am still okay even in the weakest moment of my life. As much as this hurts, something beautiful is slowly blossoming here: the understanding that NO ONE can give me the strength and NO ONE can take this journey *except me.*

I curl up in the hotel room bed and sleep for one hour before starting my drive back to face reality in Countryhaven. I look very closely at Pittsburgh's roads, at Pittsburgh's bridges, at Pittsburgh's buildings and think, "I hope this is the last time I ever see these things again."

CHAPTER 25
THE WIZARD AND WALMART

My dad is sitting at our kitchen table with his best friend Tom. The fireplace crackles behind them. They are sampling something that just came out of the oven. My mom's Italian blood has served us all very well. She never stops cooking. Our house smells like a freshly baked anything pretty much always.

I sit down and join them. I want to share my plan with Tom and possibly say goodbye. Tom has white hair and a white beard and has served as a wise wizard throughout my life. He is also responsible for a childhood that smells like patchouli, my favorite scent in the world, because it's all he wears. I get the sense that he's here for moral support for my dad right now.

"Nick and I broke up. I want to move to California." I confess.

Tom looks over to my dad without so much as a pause. "Well why don't you give her a little money, Sam?"

"She doesn't know anyone in Encinitas or have a place to live." My dad's face is so somber it hurts me.

"I'll be fine, Dad. I've been traveling my whole life."

Then the wizard says, "At least you have a dream, Morgan. Most people just sit around here, too scared of dreaming of anything different."

I don't think my dad can believe his response. Neither can I, but it gives me the fuel I need to make it through the evening.

Until we go to Walmart.

My sister needs some sort of supply for school. I don't really hear what it is but know that it doesn't seem important enough for a trip to Walmart. I ask my parents if I can stay in the car. The answer is no. So I slowly maneuver myself, hood up, out of the car with my mom, dad, and sister. The automatic doors make way to the smells of chemicals and plastic. I shuffle my feet over the cold white floors that the fluorescent light hits so harshly, that I slip into a walking coma. I question a bright green-colored tank top for my apparent move to California when a song I know very well comes on. It's our song, me and Nick. Is this a sign? This has got to be the weakest I've felt, maybe ever. I set the tank top down. I'm only putting things in my parents' cart that I actually need which doesn't seem like much right now.

Of course we run into people we know within two minutes. I have no makeup on and the darkest colored hoodie I could find. I think I have pants on too but I don't remember. I pretend that I am invisible and it seems to be working. But their words are penetrating my ears nonetheless. What they are talking about is none other than their daughter (who happened to be in my high school graduating class) who just had her first baby. She's married and living in a nice cul-de-sac in Barraine. Could this be any more of a house of horrors? A broken down Walmart on a rainy night where I'm already questioning my sanity.

The shopping is over and even though I'm numb, I can still feel the blistering cold wind as we walk to the car.

CHAPTER 26
WHO'S INSANE: ME OR THEM?

Day five of living at home and I'm sick. Literally. I'm not sleeping, every waking moment is filled with the highest amounts of stress possible, and I'm trying to put together a plan that my parents keep batting down as illogical. Plus, I'm trying to keep up with my school work.

I'm lying in bed listening to the founder of my school talk about preparing kale when suddenly his lecture takes quite a different direction:

"We make a plan for our life. We set things up in a way that makes our future predictable. We have a pretty good idea what our lives will look like in one year from now or five years from now. We also have choice. We can also say 'Fuck it.'"

Boom, baby. That intense conviction makes me forget that I'm sick and I get back on my research about Encinitas.

Following Claire's suggestion, I call her father. My Uncle John has been a lifelong mentor, quite possibly because he is someone who never quite took the traditional route in his own life. I tell him the story from start to finish. I tell him my dream.

"Am I crazy, Uncle John?"

"What you are saying to me doesn't sound crazy. In fact, sometimes the craziest ideas are the best ones. Actually, Morgan, you sound to me like a pioneer. We just want you to be safe. I suggest you put together an actual strategic plan for your move."

I begin the process of putting together my strategic plan on my new laptop that my mom just bought me. In the middle of my research I notice something in the kitchen: my sister. Eighteen years old. Full of life. What kind of role model do I want to be for her? What advice would I give to her in this situation? That's pretty simple:

"What do you want to do in the world? Do it."

I can't give up now. That story would be tragic:

Morgan had this dream that she wanted to move somewhere she loved so she broke up with her boyfriend and attempted to plan the move only to back out and then went on living a life she only half wanted.

No. I could puke in my mouth. That thought is disgusting. If my sister had a dream, I'd tell her to follow it. Period. What are these limitations we've placed upon ourselves anyways? They aren't even real. Who's insane? Is it me or is it them?

Chapter 27
Stay Strong

Today it's me that's the insane one, I believe.

March 17, 2014

> *Do I love Nick? Yes. Do I want to be with him? No. I can't trust myself. I change my mind All The Time about important things like love and spending my life with someone. It's not love! In what universe is love able to say, "I'm leaving because you hold me back." How could I stay with someone who I think does that? He says I hold myself back. To that I say yes, I do. But I hold myself back by being afraid to do anything else besides date you. I would've preferred that Dex said, "Stay in that relationship with Nick - it is good for you." That would've been far, far easier. I wanted Dex's message. It could've been because I'm so clearly indecisive or because it's what I needed to hear. Am I self-sabotaging or inspired? I want to be guided by Truth but to most importantly be able to pick up what is True! I need to meditate.*

After twenty minutes of silence in my blue meditation chair I hear a knock on my door,

"Dreama would like to meet with you."

My mom has arranged a meeting with a friend of the family who I've never met. She lives in California and happens to be in town this week. If I'm really going to move, she wants someone who is able to offer guidance about the area.

I pull into Giant Eagle and walk into the cafe. As soon as I see her, I know I'm going to cry. She is the sweetest woman I have ever seen. Short brown curly hair, glasses and the presence of compassion that I can feel before she even utters a word.

Tucked into the corner booth of our neighborhood grocery store, I begin to tell her the story.

For five minutes, I tell her everything I can about Nick.

"He is a good man. He wanted to make a life with me. And we have a certain chemistry together."

She waits and then begins her response.

"The chemistry isn't relevant. He's not the one."

Her conviction alongside this answer sends the biggest rush of relief through my body.

Then I tell her everything I can about Dex.

"He's been a mentor to me. He's shown me things I never knew I could see."

She begins, "He thinks differently than everyone else but he's not the one either."

My whole body relaxes.

"When you meet the one, it will be very different than these relationships. It's pretty simple. When you know, you know."

Those words are familiar to me, but I still don't know what it is "to know."

I ponder this for a moment then continue.

"I'm not sure if this makes any sense, Dreama, but there has to be room for something bigger to come through. It doesn't feel like that can happen here. I can't take the chance of staying and not finding out."

"It makes complete sense to me."

I tell her about California. How I want to move to Encinitas with no job, home, or car and without knowing anybody there.

"Everyone's afraid for me, but I think I can make it."

"You'll make it! Of course you'll make it! This is your dream, Morgan, no one else's, and you have to go!"

My God, what a weight lifted. "Thank you Dreama! Thank you so much!"

"Remember, Morgan, this will be the hardest part when everyone is disagreeing with your decision. Stay strong right now."

I pull out of the parking lot with an expansive feeling in my chest. I have been asking for a sign for days. This was the sign. And it just happens to be the sign that I wanted to see all along.

CHAPTER 28
NO LOOKING BACK

Nights are the hardest. Mornings are the easiest. When I feel good and happy, I want to follow through with my plan. When I feel sad or tired, I want to stay. Luckily I have somewhere to be today: a dentist appointment in Pittsburgh. Going anywhere, being in motion, is better than sitting still right now.

I have a cavity which is the scariest thing I can think of for a multitude of reasons. First of all, I have welfare dental insurance. Welfare dental insurance is the only type of insurance you can get when you're 28 and you earn $1,000 per month. Second of all, I have never met this doctor in my life. And third, they are trying to use metal to fill the cavity. I've always been an avid researcher on all things health, and I've known for a long time that having metal in the mouth is a big no-no. Staking my claim here means more to me than looking like a weirdo in front of a dentist I'll never see again.

"Do you have anything other than metal to fill the filling?" I ask the dentist prepared to walk out of the room if she says no.

She looks at me for a second like, who is this person? Then she tells me she can fill it with composite. A victory for me.

There's a needle going into my gums and I'm saying lightning fast Hail Marys in my head. Minutes later I open my eyes and breathe again. The procedure is over. This may have been the easiest cavity I've ever had filled. I'm thanking God for these people right now, for health and assurance of my decisions.

As if I hadn't already gotten my sign, I'm always open to more reassurance. My jumping mind is silenced as soon as I walk out to pay the $25 that I owe. Something makes me peer behind the receptionist desk. My eyes focus in on a coffee mug sitting amid a stack of papers. It only takes a moment to realize that written in big red letters on the mug is the word: "CALIFORNIA."

The sign on the mug provides me with about 30 minutes of peace on my drive home. But when the sign for Barraine comes up, I've completely lost my mind. At 31 minutes I find myself putting my right turn signal on. By minute 32, I'm in Barraine. Then, since it's lunchtime, I'm pulling into the parking lot of our restaurant.

I park my car to face the restaurant. I look around the parking lot, and just as expected, his truck is here, too. This has been our daily lunch spot since we opened the office. I'm parked far enough away that he can't see me, but close enough that I can see him. My heart pounds as I spot his right side profile in the center booth. My heart goes from pounding to breaking when

I realize that he is alone. There is an empty spot to his left where I used to sit. Nick sits, by himself, eating lunch.

What have I done to this man? His life? What kind of person am I to leave him here alone? I keep my eyes on him watching every movement.

I don't know why I'm here. Maybe to see this? Maybe to ask for forgiveness? He stands up to put on his leather coat. He walks to the door, out into the cold, towards his truck. His key goes into his ignition...

My door swings open, "Nick!"

He didn't expect me here. I know this from the look on his face which displays a mix of both hope and pain. I walk to him. I reach my arms out towards this strong man and grasp him tightly. He doesn't fight it. His body softens, allowing me in again. I always felt so safe wrapped up with him, even now. I pull back to look at his eyes, attempting to communicate with him nonverbally just how sorry I am.

"Look, uh, I don't know why I'm here. It's cold. Do you want to sit in the car for a minute?"

"No, I really don't, Morgan."

"Please Nick, just for a minute."

We walk over to my car and shut the doors. Even though it's cold, the sun shines on my face. I wish it wouldn't. I wish he couldn't see me right now.

"So it's kind of hard for me to talk and my face looks funny because it's numb. I just had a cavity filled."

He looks at me with compassion in his eyes. I am so surprised that he has any of that left for me.

"You can't even notice," he says and his voice is kind.

"I just wanted to say I'm sorry. Again. I just wanted to make sure you were okay."

"I mean I'm okay. That doesn't mean this isn't hard or that it doesn't hurt." He rolls his window down. I'm not quite sure why.

"I wish it wasn't. I wish it didn't hurt at all. I wish I could take it away for you."

"Well, you can come stay with me. For just one more night."

I ponder my heart. I know that he's hurting. I know it would help for the night. I know it would hurt in the long run. One night back in Scenic Hill could change the course of history.

Very softly I begin, "I'm moving to California next week. I think staying together would only make things harder."

The compassion leaves his face. His pain turns into a more protective emotion: anger. Before I know it things are starting to get escalated in the car.

"You shouldn't have come, Morgan."

"I'm sorry Nick. I really am. I wish I'd known!"

The passenger door closes. His pounding steps crush the salt on the blacktop beneath him. As he opens his truck door I watch the steam from his words rise in the air as he repeats it again,

"You shouldn't have come."

CHAPTER 29
SECOND THOUGHTS

March 26, 2014

There is a part of me that's secretly excited and not scared. Nick said going was selfish. I do think it is, but I'm going to try to make my life better. I'm also going because I've always wanted to. That may be the selfish part. No. The selfish part is not being in tune with what I actually want and choosing fear and security over that. There's something exciting about only taking what you need and not knowing exactly where you're going...except you know you're going somewhere. Scrape by. That might be what I want to prove to myself. That I can do it.

"Morgan, how rational is this? You don't know anybody in Encinitas. You don't have a place to live. You don't have a car. And you don't have job. How do you expect me to feel right now? You need to at least figure out the living situation and the job before you go." My mom repeats her very logical argument for the hundredth time.

I shoot a quick email to Dex:

> "I should leave ASAP. Parents are really stressed about my decision and I need to be able to focus. Will you be in Pittsburgh tomorrow for me to swing by? The longer I'm here, the harder it will be for me to go."

I don't know how much money Dex is giving me but I don't care. I'll make any amount work. I just want to go soon.

I've spent 24 hours on Craigslist searching for jobs and apartments. Not having either of these things is not going to stop me. One thing seems certain: it will be a lot easier for me to find both once I arrive in Encinitas. This mindset, however, is quite concerning to my family members who care about me.

I promised to make Italian cookies with my aunt before I go. Without saying it, we know that this is her attempt to make sure I'm okay and to try to convince me to wait to move until I have things in order. Without saying it, I know this is my way of saying goodbye.

My aunt's home is one of those houses that always smells like a home with the familiar scents of garlic and tomato sauce cooked into the walls. On maybe our 200th pizzelle, my cousin walks in with his four-year-old son. The smell of the warm cookies, my laughing little cousin, the smiles on my aunt and uncle's faces…this unexpectedly disarms me. I realize something about myself. There's a part of me that wants this so bad, too. My heart would really love a family.

How could I leave all of this? I had the chance for a family right in front of me but I walked away. This could all be mine. The search could be over. Oh, how comfortable and warm and safe I could be in my nice home in Barraine with my handsome and successful husband with my family right down the road. I could beg on my hands and knees and then have this all back. I may never get this chance again. *Don't you remember how long you looked for this and the years of pain it took to find it?*

There are so many things I could say to him right now that would make this all go away. My life could be so easy here. And there would be love too. *Don't forget. Nick loves you. He's displayed it in his actions since day one.* All I would have to do is call him and apologize. Would he even take me back at this point? I could run back, drop to my knees and beg for forgiveness. I could tell him I made a mistake. We could move into a new house together. I could continue to work from his office. I can be more respectful. I promise. I could tell him that I won't talk to Dex anymore. We can get married and start trying to have kids. I'll be okay with only vacationing to warm spots a few times a year. I'll cook and I'll clean. Maybe I could even learn to enjoy this life in Barraine…

CHAPTER 30
LEAVING DREAM LAND

Dex replies to my email at 1:07 p.m.:

"I can meet you in Pittsburgh tonight at 9."

With that meeting locked in I find my flight. The earliest flight that leaves tomorrow is the one I'm taking. Why wait?

I call my dad.

"Dad, I'm taking the 6:30 a.m. flight tomorrow. Where are you?"

I drive back the long dirt road to my father's oasis: The Farm. The Farm is a 100-acre green plot of expansive land with historic barns and Western Pennsylvania charm. The Farm was my favorite place in the world when I was seven. At that time, it was owned by an old man who kept every type of animal and every type of baby animal imaginable on site. Horses and colts. Cats and kittens. Dogs and puppies. Goats and kids. It was little Morgan's dream land. I asked my dad to take me to The Farm every day.

Now, 20 years later, my dad has bought this land with its barns and magic from the old farmer. The Farm became a spot for my dad's own personal creative expression. He cleaned up the old barns and made them habitable. Many hours were spent in "The Granary" where my dad created a homemade wooden bar and bar stools, hung buffalo heads, deer antlers and fish trophies for him and his buddies to drink beer.

But as I pulled closer I could feel it before he even turned to face me. This tough guy I had forever admired had been crying. My heart jumps and melts and hurts all at once. I think of just days earlier during a discussion about my move when he said, "You can live here forever with us." And the hardest thing in the world for me to realize is that my dream has ramifications that look like my father crying.

We didn't say much. He showed me some progress he had made on one of the old buildings. I swallowed the pain in my throat knowing that it would be a long time before I made another trip down this dusty dirt road to see him. I breathed in the site of the wide-open grassland that little Morgan had adored more than anywhere in the world. I saw her sitting on top of the dried hay bales petting a newborn puppy. I watched her run through the pastures with the horses that always seemed too wild to tame. I saw her daddy watching her run, never expecting that she would run too far away. And she never really did. Until now.

They walked through her childhood paradise, her daddy's adult paradise, knowing that they no longer shared the same paradise anymore. Tomorrow, she would go on her quest to find her new home. The place that she knew of in her heart but couldn't explain with her mind. She prayed to God that she would not break her father's heart because she loved him more than any man in the world.

CHAPTER 31
IT IS TIME

Up the long winding road I reach a place where the heartbeat of the walls pounds with our memories. Thousands of moments in this dark, creaking condo shifted the course of my entire life. I place my car in park and like so many times before, wait.

Ten minutes later headlights shine on the bushes and a sleek, black vehicle pulls in beside me. I step of out of my car and stand awaiting him. He hands me a piece of paper. I look down to see a check made out to Morgan River for $4,000. I place it on the driver's seat and look up at him,

"Thank you."

I reach for him and he falls into my arms, sobbing. I've ached for this moment, to feel him in the flesh, to be close to him again. Not just now, but for so much of our relationship I've ached for the very same thing.

Wrapping him in my arms, I stand very still for five minutes, aware that if I move he may stop crying. I don't want him to stop crying until he feels better. I don't want him to stop crying until he's ready.

He pulls back from my shoulder and we look at each other. There are so many things I don't understand about this man. God knows I've tried to grasp the way he sees the world, the people in it, and the way he leads his life. But I really don't.

I tell him about my dream, "I had a dream that we were at the ocean together."

"I pictured us at the ocean together today too."

"Really?"

"Yes."

I fill with hope in this moment that maybe things could be different for us in California. Maybe our lives could be very simple. Maybe we could get this thing right. Dex reads my mind and intervenes.

"I need you to realize something, Morgan. We may never see each other again after tonight. We may never talk again. You don't need me in your ear anymore. It is your time."

There is nothing more to do, to say, to feel. There is nothing to argue, nothing to reconcile. Goodbye is all there is. This man has released me here tonight.

Northbound again. Dark, cold night again. Goodbye, Dex. Goodbye, Nick. Goodbye, Cash, Rich and every single man I've dated. Thank you for being my facilitator for change.

Goodbye, Pittsburgh. Thank you for stoking the soul flame – allowing me the courage to leave you and go.

CHAPTER 32
EVERYTHING WILL BE OKAY

I quietly finish packing then lie down, eyes wide open. The walls of my small bedroom are filled with things that aren't quite customary in Countryhaven. A picture of the beautiful Hindu goddess Saraswati gracefully perched atop a swan, a Hare Krishna mantra, books about reincarnation, astral planes and a God that can be accessed within each and every person. When all else was lost for me, I could always be lifted by these reminders that there is much, much more going on than meets the eye and that it is all really very lovely.

I hug my stuffed animal, Puffalump, who I've had since I was two. He's not coming along this time. When my mother walks in the door at 2:30 a.m. I awaken from a light sleep and welcome her in. When she lies down I realize that she is trembling and crying. I hold her beside me and we fall asleep together in my bed with my favorite cream-colored bamboo sheets.

At 3:30 a.m. my alarm reminds me of the world I am leaving. This is the hardest thing I've ever done. The strength to move my body comes from something I've never accessed.

I watch it all happen: my dad taking my luggage, my sister crying, my puppy sleeping. I lie in my sister's warm bed. I can feel the gratitude of ten-year-old Morgan receiving her wish after years of begging for it: a little sister. I can feel the love bursting forth for her and my brother who is now living his life in New York.

"Everything is going to be okay. Believe in me." I say those words to her. She says she does. I can feel it.

I can barely stand letting go of the little warm eight-pound body of our puppy. I hold her so close to my chest. She is responsible for opening my heart so much wider in the five years that she's graced our family.

I look back at my childhood bedroom for the tenth time and then shut the door. Of all the possessions I have collected inside this room over the years, I've chosen only what can fit into two suitcases.

The exits on the freeway fly by as my dad drives and my mom speaks. One hour in the car and the big metal wings come into plain view. One minute and we will be at Departures.

Vanilla body cream. Cucumber face soap. The most vivid childhood smells of my mother. Six years old, "Mommy don't leave me. Please!" She will get on the airplane today to go to work but I wish we could spend forever together. I refuse to get out of her car. But apparently, kids have to go to school. Through the doorway, I feel very alone in my sadness. My teacher is wearing vanilla. I cry on my desk, hiding from the other students. Separation anxiety.

Today, age 28, I walk away but I do not cry. I step out of her car 22 years later, and this time, I am the one who is comforting her. Because just like the woman who I watched live her dream as a flight attendant, her daughter has a dream also. And it takes an airplane to get to that dream as well.

Hugs. Goodbye. I love you. I glance back but I cannot turn around. I keep moving in the direction of that dream. The sliding glass airport doors pull me in. I walk through the security line. I walk to the airplane away from my mom, from my dad, and 22 years later, I do not feel alone.

CHAPTER 33
MARCH 28, 2014

The airplane exhaust smells like freedom. I look down at the Earth. I feel powerful way up here. I am traveling 500 miles per hour towards my new life. I close my eyes and remember a vision I had years ago on an airplane, of Mary as a figure of light behind my closed eyes.

How could I have known to take this journey? How could I have known to travel 2,500 miles west to a place I've never been? Up here, so high, with a bird's eye view of it all, it doesn't seem so crazy anymore.

The grey clouds make way for the light. I touch my window. The ice has melted. All thoughts, worries and emotions have left me. The red mountains below, the iridescent white clouds. I am in awe of it all.

"Welcome to paradise," the pilot announces over the speaker. The sun is the only thing I see as we touch down. The sun is the reality I choose now. I step into the San Diego air, and for the first time in my life I am completely alone. And it feels freaking amazing.

I find a driver with a van and I tell him I'm going to the Days Inn in Encinitas. He pulls away from the curb. Here we are, in motion! I see the boats and the water and my God, do people really live here?

The I-5 is next. I'm staring at the ocean as we cruise along. I've never been on such a beautiful interstate in my life. I'm already inspired!

There is no time anymore as we glide along the highway, only pure exhilaration. Pure presence. Pure freedom.

2 miles Encinitas Boulevard.

What will it be like? What will I see? What will I learn? Who will I meet?

1 mile Encinitas Boulevard.

The driver takes the exit then turns left and says,

"Really everything you need to explore is this way, to the west, towards the ocean."

My heart jumps in my chest. For the first time in my life I know who I am. I'm the girl who allowed herself to be weak so she would know what it meant to be strong.

I love that girl.
I love that person.
I love that me who did all those things.
Everything I did.
I love it all.
It all brought me here.

83114412R00080

Made in the USA
Columbia, SC
23 December 2017